ALEX RIDER

STORMBREAKER™

Starring:

Sarah Bolger		as Sabina Pleasure
Robbie Coltrane		as the Prime Minister
Stephen Fry		as Smithers
Damian Lewis		as Yassen Gregorovich
Ewan McGregor		as Ian Rider
Bill Nighy		as Alan Blunt
Sophie Okonedo		as Mrs. Jones
Alex Pettyfer		as Alex Rider
Missi Pyle		as Nadia Vole
Andy Serkis		as Mr. Grin
Alicia Silverstone		as Jack Starbright
Ashley Walters		as Wolf
	and	
Mickey Rourke		as Darrius Sayle

ALEX RIDER

STORMBREAKER™

THE OFFICIAL SCRIPT

ANTHONY HOROWITZ

speak

An Imprint of Penguin Group (USA) Inc.

SPEAK
Published by the Penguin Group
Penguin Group(USA) Inc.,
345 Hudson Street, New York, New York 10014, U.S.A.
Penguin Group (Canada), 90 Eglinton Avenue East, Suite 700,
Toronto, Ontario, Canada M4P 2Y3
(a division of Pearson Penguin Canada Inc.)
Penguin Books Ltd, 80 Strand, London WC2R 0RL, England
Penguin Ireland, 25 St Stephen's Green, Dublin 2, Ireland
(a division of Penguin Books Ltd)
Penguin Group (Australia), 250 Camberwell Road,
Camberwell, Victoria 3124, Australia
(a division of Pearson Australia Group Pty Ltd)
Penguin Books India Pvt Ltd, 11 Community Centre, Panchsheel Park,
New Delhi - 110 017, India
Penguin Group (NZ), Cnr Airborne and Rosedale Roads,
Albany, Auckland 1310, New Zealand
(a division of Pearson New Zealand Ltd)
Penguin Books (South Africa) (Pty) Ltd, 24 Sturdee Avenue,
Rosebank, Johannesburg 2196, South Africa

Registered Offices: Penguin Books Ltd, 80 Strand,
London WC2R 0RL, England

First published in the United States of America by Speak,
an imprint of Penguin Group(USA) Inc. 2006

1   3   5   7   9   10   8   6   4   2

Copyright © Samuelsons / IoM Film, 2006

Speak ISBN 0-14-240730-5
Printed in the United States of America

I'm not quite sure exactly what you're holding in your hand right now.

Between April 2003 and June 2005, when we began shooting *Alex Rider: Stormbreaker™*, I wrote fourteen different drafts of the screenplay. This is quite normal when you're making a big-budget movie. In that time, I was receiving notes from the producers, Marc Samuelson and Peter Samuelson, from the director, Geoff Sax, and from financers in the UK, America, and the Isle of Man. Believe it or not, I was still writing the film just a few days earlier this week (it's now February 2006 and filming finished four months ago—but we still needed to add some O/S dialogue, which is to say words you hear spoken but don't see).

In other words, this version of the screenplay may differ in some respects from the finished film. To get this book printed and into the shops in time for the launch, we simply couldn't wait any longer, although I hope it is very close to the finished movie. I visited the film set many times and saw for myself how quickly things could change.

Some scenes were dropped simply because the director ran out of time. Blowing up the fish tank, for example, took twice as long as anyone had expected (they used several pounds of Semtex!) and that meant losing a whole chunk of the morning and, with it, half a scene of the script.

Sometimes actors found different ways of interpreting what I'd written. A good example of this is the Smithers scene. Stephen Fry added a couple of great jokes that I'm more than happy to take credit for. They helped him develop the character, but they were never in the original script.

And once they moved from the set to the cutting room, the film mutated at an even greater speed.

Everything was trimmed. Scenes were put in new places. Other scenes hit the famous "cutting room floor." The first time I saw the film it was 120 minutes long. By the end, it was just over 90 minutes long...and all the better for it. Things that had worked, and seemed either funny or exciting when we were shooting them, were just too slow for the finished film. They had to go. There were bits that made no sense. Other bits that went on too long. Editing the film was like making a sculpture. The editor kept chipping away until the shape emerged.

I still haven't seen the finished, locked-off, final version of the film so I can't point to the script and tell you which parts of it have survived unscathed. But this script is as close as we could get and I hope you will enjoy it as both a souvenir of the movie and as an example of "work in progress."

Over two hundred people worked on *Alex Rider: Stormbreaker*™. But this is where it all began.

—Anthony Horowitz
February 2006

1   **INT.   BROOKLAND SCHOOL - CLASS   DAY.**   1

A good-looking fourteen-year-old BOY is looking at us, sitting at his desk. We might think this is ALEX RIDER...

> TEACHER
> (voice only)
> What is it that makes us
> what we are?

...but the CAMERA is already moving. Past two more BOYS.

> TEACHER
> (voice only)
> What is it that defines us?
> Is it where we live? Is it
> our schooling?

The CAMERA passes several more fourteen-year-olds: BOYS and GIRLS.

> TEACHER
> (voice only)
> Or is it our family?

And at last the CAMERA pulls focus to reveal a BOY four rows behind. His head is down, concentrating on his work.

> TEACHER
> (voice only)
> Alex Rider. Family. Have you
> prepared something for us?

Hearing his name, ALEX RIDER looks up. He's also fourteen. Stylishly dressed - there's no uniform at this school. Very fit. Very good-looking. Can a fourteen-year-old be sexy? The girls in the class think one is.

                    ALEX
          (Unwilling) Yes.

                    TEACHER
          Come on, then.

ALEX walks to the front, holding an essay. As he goes, he catches the eye of a pretty fourteen-year-old girl - SABINA PLEASURE. She is becoming more interested in him by the moment.

ALEX has joined the TEACHER, who is himself young, good-looking, dedicated. Above all, on the KIDS' side. Standing at the front, ALEX faces the entire class.

                    TEACHER
          Go on...

                    ALEX
          Yeah. OK.

ALEX pauses. Very reluctant. The TEACHER nods, encouraging him. ALEX'S brief synopsis disguises a life with a certain emptiness...

                    ALEX
          There's not much I can say
          about my family. (Beat) I
          didn't even know my parents.
          They died when I was small.
          I live with my uncle and
          he's not there much either.
          I have a sort of housekeeper
          because he's always away on
          business. He's got a really
          boring job.

CUT TO:

2 **EXT.   HI-TECH FACTORY   DAY.**   2

An explosion. A fireball of flame. IAN
RIDER bursts out of a warehouse on a
sleek, powerful MOTORBIKE. Alarms go off.
He's pursued by four more MOTORBIKES. The
pursuers are shooting at IAN RIDER,
machine-gun fire strafes the ground as he
makes his escape.

> ALEX
> (voice only)
> He's a bank supervisor. He's
> in charge of customer care.

An ARMED GUARD stands in RIDER'S way. RIDER
lashes out with a foot. The GUARD crumples.

CUT TO:

3 **INT.   BROOKLAND SCHOOL - CLASS   DAY.**   3

ALEX is still reading his essay to the
class. And he still isn't enjoying it.

> ALEX
> His work means a lot to him
> but he never talks about it.
> So that's about it. The End.

ALEX stops. SABINA is watching him closely. Next
to her, a boy called GARY notices her attention
and scowls. The TEACHER is nonplussed.

> TEACHER
> Is that it, Alex?

> ALEX
> Yeah.

> TEACHER
> It wasn't quite as insightful
> as I'd hoped. Where is your
> uncle now?

                    ALEX
He's at some sort of con-
ference.

                    TEACHER
Oh yes? And what that's
about?

                                        CUT TO:

4   **EXT.   CORNISH ROADS   DAY.**   4

IAN RIDER screams down a Cornish road. The
four chasing BIKES are right behind him.
Getting closer and closer. Firing at him.
The BIKES pass perilously close but he
manages to avoid them. Fast cuts. His face,
his front wheel, the chasing bikes, the
road...just a blur. Now he is screaming
down a coastal road, a sheer drop to one
side, the pursuers gaining on him.

                    ALEX
              (voice only)
        "New approaches to European
        banking. Life in the slow
        lane."

One pulls alongside and tries to knock him
off but IAN RIDER manages to pull away.
Ahead of him, a sign: PORT TALLON WELCOMES
CAREFUL DRIVERS. He goes past it so fast,
the sign rocks in the wind.

It rocks four more times as the other BIKERS
pass by. Then collapses to one side.

                                        CUT TO:

5   **EXT.   SEAWALL   DAY.**   5

IAN RIDER comes to a seawall...and keeps
going. His BIKE leaps into the air, hangs
there for a moment, then arcs down onto the
sand. Two of the BIKERS follow. One gets
the angle wrong and crashes, a spinning
ball of sand and screaming metal.

                                              CUT TO:

6   **EXT.   BEACH   DAY.**   6

Now IAN RIDER is speeding along the sand,
following the curve of the sea. The following BIKER produces a machine pistol and
fires. The sand spits up around him.

Two SEAGULLS watch him pass, their heads
snapping round.

PUNCH & JUDY watch him pass, their heads
snapping round.

A MOTORBOAT cuts in from the sea, surges
through the water, and rockets across the
beach. The crew fires BAZOOKAS and great
mounds of sand leap up, just missing IAN RIDER.

ANOTHER ANGLE. Farther along the beach.
There's no way through. BIKERS have blocked
the way - they're waiting with guns.

There's an upside-down boat, propped up to one
side. IAN RIDER slides underneath it. He hits
the props holding up the boat and it falls down
on top of him, forming a protective shield.

A second later, the BIKERS spray the boat
with machine-gun fire. The bullets can't
reach IAN RIDER. For the moment, he's safe.

7   **INT.   BROOKLAND SCHOOL - CLASS   DAY.**   7

A sudden cut back to ALEX.

                    ALEX
          The thing about my uncle
          is, he's not very easy to
          pin down.

                                              CUT TO:

8   **EXT.   BEACH   DAY.**   8

The BIKERS heave the boat back up on its

side. IAN RIDER'S motorbike is there. But impossibly, he has gone.

On the road above - a REVVING SOUND. THE BIKERS look up as a glinting tiger of a sports car screeches away.

IAN RIDER is safe now. He clicks his seat belt on, then speeds out of the town...

CUT TO:

8A   **INT.   BROOKLAND SCHOOL   -   CLASS DAY.**   8A

Alex finishes his essay.
>   ALEX
>   I wouldn't say I was much
>   like him. And I don't think
>   anyone makes us what we
>   are. I think we just are...

9   **EXT.   CORNISH ROAD   DAY.**   9

CLOSE SHOT on the number plate of the car: R1D3R. It's speeding away into the distance.

IAN RIDER continues to drive, putting distance between himself and the village. He looks in his mirror and sees the two MOTORCYCLISTS coming up fast behind.

And he thought it was all over! But it's easily dealt with. IAN RIDER presses a button. The CD PLAYER in the car flips over to show a TV monitor and a command: REAR MISSILES. The TV monitor displays two blips-RADAR - the bikes coming up fast behind.

IAN RIDER glances at the screen. He waits for the AUTOMATIC GUIDANCE SYSTEM to lock on, then reaches out and almost casually presses down. Two MISSILES - barely glimpsed - fire out of the back of his car.

He drives on. Over the brow of the hill. Far behind him, unseen, there are two explosions.

And at the same time, THE RINGING OF A BELL...

CUT TO:

10 **INT.   BROOKLAND SCHOOL - CLASS   DAY.** 10

The bell signals the end of the lesson.
Desks slam. ALEX RIDER, SABINA PLEASURE,
and the rest of the class leave cheerfully,
noisily. The TEACHER calls after them.

>TEACHER
>Alex, that was terrible!

CUT TO:

11 **INT.   BROOKLAND SCHOOL - CORRIDOR   DAY.** 11

ALEX RIDER and about a dozen SCHOOL KIDS
stream out into the corridor. There's a
poster on the wall. THE NEW STORMBREAKER.
YOUR SCHOOL WILL HAVE ONE SOON.

SABINA PLEASURE is among them. GARY is with
her. GARY is not exactly a bully. But he's
a hunk who fancies SABINA and throws his
weight around to prove it.

>GARY
>(Mocking) That was really sad
>about having no mum and dad,
>Alex. You're such a loser!

>SABINA
>Why don't you just get
>lost, Gary?

ALEX is surprised that SABINA has turned
on GARY. So is GARY.

>SABINA
>Bullies are so...last year.

She walks off. ALEX and GARY exchange a
look. ALEX can't quite believe his luck.
Does the prettiest girl in the school
fancy him?

CUT TO:

12   **EXT.   BROOKLAND SCHOOL   DAY.**   12

SABINA walks across the school yard. Loads of
other SCHOOL KIDS are leaving at the end
of the day.

In fact this is ALEX'S POV. He's standing
with his bike, watching SABINA. Does he
dare move in on her? He makes a decision
and hurries forward.

ANOTHER ANGLE. SABINA reaches the school
gate. And ALEX is already there, waiting
nonchalantly, somehow disguising the fact
he sprinted ahead of her.

                    ALEX
        Hey...

                    SABINA
        Alex...

                    ALEX
        (Unsure) I was wondering.
        Do you want to do something
        this weekend?

                    SABINA
        No.

ALEX'S face falls. SABINA takes pity on him.

                    SABINA
        I can't. I have riding les-
        sons on Saturday and then I'm
        going out with my mum and dad.

She remembers that ALEX has just been
speaking about having no mum and dad...

                    SABINA
        Sorry...

                    ALEX
        No. It doesn't matter.

                    SABINA
        Maybe next weekend.

                    ALEX
        Whatever.

ALEX stands, a little deflated, as SABINA
walks away. Then his CELL PHONE rings.

                              CUT TO:

13 **EXT.   CORNISH ROAD   DAY.**   13

IAN RIDER is driving along a long, straight
road. And he's safe! He's called ALEX on
his hands-free.

                    IAN
        Hey - Alex?

                              CUT TO:

14 **EXT.   ROADS ADJACENT TO BROOKLAND SCHOOL/**   14
        CORNISH ROAD   DAY.

ALEX is cycling home. He stops to take the call
on his cell phone. He is really pleased to hear
from IAN RIDER. From here, we CUT BETWEEN THEM.

                    ALEX
        Are you coming home?

                    IAN
        Yeah - I'm on my way now.

                    ALEX
        How was the conference?

                    IAN
        It was fine. You know how
        they are.

                    ALEX
        No, I don't. You never tell me.

                    IAN
        There's nothing to tell.

Look - I'm really sorry about
last week. I know I said I'd
be there. But this trip just
came out of nowhere...

          ALEX
Same as always.

          IAN
Yeah. But I'll be back for
dinner and then we've got
the whole weekend.

          ALEX
(Wary) Really?

          IAN
Come on! When did I ever
let you down?

          ALEX
You want me to answer that?

          IAN
Yeah, I know. I'll see you
soon. OK?

          ALEX
I'm glad you called.

          IAN
Me too.

IAN smiles and hangs up. He presses a button and the CD PLAYER twists back into
place. The car is filled with classical
music. IAN RIDER drives on, doing about
seventy. And then...

Out of nowhere. Impossibly. There's a man seem-
ingly flying next to the window upside down.
The man is blond-haired, superfit, built like
a ballet dancer. Aged in his late thirties.

This is YASSEN GREGOROVICH. Russia's dead-
liest assassin. Death itself. And he's
right next to the car.

ANOTHER ANGLE - and we see how it's done. YASSEN is dangling out of a helicopter that's flying overhead. The classical music drowns out the sound of the rotors.

There's nothing IAN RIDER can do. YASSEN GREGOROVICH reaches behind him. He stretches his arms as if crucified, then brings them together. Only now he's holding automatic pistols.

He fires. The bullets travel toward the camera, toward the cinema screen. They arrive and the whole screen shatters like glass, the pieces falling in slow motion, twisting and turning.

15   **OPENING CREDITS**   15

                                              FADE TO:

16   **EXT.   IAN RIDER'S HOUSE   DAY.**   16

ALEX bikes down a smart road in Chelsea, West London, with his books in a bag on his back. Georgian terraced houses. This is where he lives.

SUDDEN DANGER. A CLOSE SHOT on a pair of female hands picking up a deadly-looking Japanese dagger. Slowly withdrawing the blade. It's razor-sharp.

                                              CUT TO:

17   **INT.   IAN RIDER'S HOUSE - HALL   DAY.**   17

ALEX lets himself into the house. He throws down his school bag and hangs up his jacket.

                     ALEX
          (Calling) Jack? I'm back...

CLOSE SHOT. The knife comes all the way out of the scabbard. We hear the blade cut the air. Then we PULL BACK and see...

18   **INT.   IAN RIDER'S HOUSE - KITCHEN   DAY.**   18

A young, very beautiful, but quite possibly lethal WOMAN is holding the knife. She raises it with intense concentration. She is wearing a kimono and Japanese headband.

                                        CUT TO:

19   **INT.   IAN RIDER'S HOUSE - HALL   DAY.**   19

ALEX suspects something is wrong. His eyes narrow. He moves slowly toward the kitchen door.

                    ALEX
          Jack?

He opens the door.

                                        CUT TO:

20   **INT.   IAN RIDER'S HOUSE - KITCHEN   DAY.**   20

The girl with the knife is JACK STARBRIGHT, an American nanny/housekeeper who looks too glamorous to be either. It would be every fourteen-year-old boy's fantasy to live with a woman like this.

She slashes down - and rather clumsily chops a tuna fish into sections. She's preparing sushi for dinner. The pieces are spread out all around her. They are all shapes and sizes...comically inept.

The next section of dialogue has subtitles in English.

                    JACK
          (In Japanese) Did you have
          a good day at school?

                    ALEX
          (In Japanese) Jack - why are
          we speaking in Japanese?

                                    JACK
                        (In Japanese) We've got a
                        special dinner tonight.
                        Sushi.

She smiles at him.

                                              CUT TO:

21 **INT.   IAN RIDER'S HOUSE - LIVING ROOM   NIGHT.** 21

ZING! A few chords of Japanese music intro-
duce us to the next scene. The living room
and the kitchen are open-plan, connected.

JACK and ALEX sit cross-legged in front of
a low table. The sushi - it looks amazing -
is between them.

                                    JACK
                        Come on, let's start. (She
                        points with her chopsticks)
                        That's salmon. Bean curd.
                        And this is the speciality
                        of the house. Fugu fish.

The FUGU FISH is like a porcupine with
spikes and a long nose.

                                    ALEX
                        Isn't that meant to be poi-
                        sonous?

                                    JACK
                        In Japan, a chef has to work
                        thirty years before they
                        let him prepare it. If you
                        don't do it exactly right
                        it'll kill you instantly.

                                    ALEX
                        How do you know you've done
                        it right?

JACK glances sideways. We see a library
book. SUSHI FOR BEGINNERS.

                         JACK
               Try the tuna...

JACK helps herself to one of the pieces.
But ALEX doesn't eat. He has no appetite.
JACK chats on to fill the silence.

                         JACK
               I've got to tell you. I met
               this amazing guy down at
               the fish shop.

                         ALEX
               (Heard it all before)
               Jack...

                         JACK
               You know the problem with this
               country? Every good-looking
               man is either married or
               gay - apart from you and you're
               too young. Come on, Alex. Have
               something!

A pause.

                         ALEX
               He's not coming, is he.

                         JACK
               Of course he is. He's proba-
               bly got caught up in traffic.

                         ALEX
               No. He'd have rung. He's
               gone to the office to put
               in a report, and the next
               thing we'll know, he'll be
               at the airport on his way to
               Hong Kong.

                         JACK
               You know his work matters
               to him.

                         ALEX
               Yeah. It matters a lot.

                    JACK
         Well, all the more for us.

JACK reaches out with her chopsticks. But
just then she hears a car draw up outside.

                    JACK
         (It's him) Hey...

Smiling, ALEX gets up and goes to open the door.

                                        CUT TO:

22   **INT.   IAN RIDER'S HOUSE - HALL   NIGHT.**   22

As ALEX approaches the door, he sees a
flashing blue light (through the glass)
and two silhouetted figures, uniformed
POLICEMEN.

                                        CUT TO:

23   **EXT.   IAN RIDER'S HOUSE   NIGHT.**   23

ALEX opens the door and we see the look in
his eyes as his entire world caves in on him.

Two uniformed POLICEMEN and a POLICE CAR
are waiting in the street. The CAMERA pulls
back...

                                        CUT TO:

24   **INT.   IAN RIDER'S HOUSE - STUDY   DAY.**   24

A picture of ALEX and IAN RIDER stands on
the desk. Taken during a mountaineering
trip. Resting, arms around shoulders. Best
friends.

Early morning. ALEX is standing in IAN
RIDER'S study, a room filled with filing
cabinets, computers, reference books, and
papers. A room full of secrets. He has
hardly ever been in here.

ALEX is wearing a dark suit, a white shirt,

and black tie. He is close to tears. But he's already cried enough. There are no more tears to come.

A movement at the door. JACK STARBRIGHT is there. She is also dressed in black.

> ALEX
> He never let me come in here. I didn't really know anything about him.

ALEX looks around him. And suddenly realizes...

> ALEX
> He was my only family, Jack. What am I going to do?

The tolling of a bell...

                                    FADE TO:

25 **EXT.   CEMETERY   DAY.**   25

A windy day. The VICAR'S robes billow around him as he speaks over the open grave.

> VICAR
> Ian Rider was a good man. Everyone who worked with him will remember him for his courage and his loyalty. He was, above all, a true patriot.

The word hits ALEX hard. The vicar just isn't talking about his uncle.

> ALEX
> (Whispered) Patriot?

Next to him, JACK shakes her head. They are among several MOURNERS. But the impression we get is not sad or somber. It's more eerie. There's something wrong.

Maybe it's ALAN BLUNT, the most senior and

influential of the mourners. Gray suit,
gray hair, steel-gray spectacles...he's as
dead as anyone in the cemetery.

Or how about MRS. JONES? BLUNT'S number two
manages to be both beautiful and slightly
sinister. A very tough, sharply dressed
woman. Eyes that never miss anything.

ALEX himself is completely out of it. Who
are all these people? Bankers? As the wind
blows and the VICAR drones on, he feels as
if he's in an episode of *The Twilight
Zone*.

He sees one of the "BANKERS" receiving a
message through an ear microphone. They
all seem pale and empty of emotion. And
then, a gust of wind catches someone's
jacket. ALEX gets only a glimpse and he's
not sure what he sees. Is that really a GUN
IN A HOLSTER? No. It's impossible...

And here's something else. A CAMERA mounted
on one of the sepulchers. Videoing the
service. It swivels toward ALEX and...

BLACK-AND-WHITE INSERT. Just for a second.
ALEX photographed. Logged. Filed away...

The VICAR winds up the service. ALEX hasn't
heard any of it.

> VICAR
> We therefore commit his
> body to the ground in sure
> and certain hope of the
> resurrection to eternal
> life. Amen.

JACK nudges him gently. The service is
over.

> JACK
> (Gently) Let's go home.

An UNDERTAKER throws a clod of earth down

toward the coffin, but before it arrives...

CUT TO: The crunch of feet on gravel. ALEX and JACK are walking out of the cemetery. One of the mourners catches up with them. His name is JOHN CRAWFORD. He's shabby and toadlike and just a little bit threatening.

> CRAWFORD
> Alex...

Nothing from ALEX.

> CRAWFORD
> My name is John Crawford. I'm with the Royal and General Bank and I want you to know you have all our condolences. It's an absolute tragedy. A car accident! If only he'd been wearing a seat belt.

> ALEX
> Thank you.

ALEX tries to walk on. But CRAWFORD hasn't finished.

> CRAWFORD
> This is Alan Blunt. He'd like a word. He's the bank chairman.

BLUNT & MRS. JONES approach.

> BLUNT
> Alex. (Beat) I'm very sorry about your uncle. We're going to miss him.

BLUNT seems to be examining ALEX as if curious about him.

> BLUNT
> He talked a lot about you.

                    ALEX
     That's strange. Because he
     never mentioned you.

                    BLUNT
     This is my deputy...Mrs. Jones.

               MRS. JONES
     I'll be in contact with you
     very soon, Alex.

                    ALEX
     Why?

               MRS. JONES
     (A little thrown) Well...
     after what's happened.
     There's the question of
     who's going to look after
     you.

                    JACK
     I'll look after him.

               MRS. JONES
     We just want to help.

                    BLUNT
     (Taking over) I'm sure
     we'll meet again, Alex.
     Hopefully somewhere a lit-
     tle less...gloomy.

BLUNT starts to walk away with MRS. JONES.
ALEX is bewildered. He has to cling to
something, to make sense of all this...

                    ALEX
     My uncle always wore his
     seat belt, Mr. Blunt. He
     was a very careful man.

BLUNT pauses. He turns around and faces ALEX.

                    BLUNT
     Not careful enough.

A brief, sad smile. BLUNT walks away.

                              CUT TO:

26   **EXT.   IAN RIDER'S HOUSE   DAY.**   26

ALEX and JACK walk back toward the house.

                    ALEX
          Did you mean what you said?
          About looking after me?

                    JACK
          Of course I did! Come on,
          Alex. You know I wouldn't
          leave you. Anyway, who else
          is there?

                    ALEX
          But will you be allowed to? I
          mean, we're not even related.

                    JACK
          I've been living with you for
          nine years. How much more
          related do you want to be?

The house comes into sight. ALEX sees TWO
MEN coming out, carrying files and other
objects from IAN'S study...including the
framed picture of ALEX and IAN. The MEN get
into a van.

                    JACK
          Was it just me or was there
          something about those bankers
          that struck you as weird...?

                    ALEX
          Jack...!

JACK sees the two men.

                    JACK
          Hey - that's all Ian's stuff!
          (Calling) What are you doing?

But as JACK hurries forward, the VAN pulls away. JACK turns around.

> JACK
>
> Alex...?

ALEX comes shooting out of the side of the house on his bicycle. He takes off, after the van.

                                    CUT TO:

27   **EXT.   LONDON STREETS   DAY.**   27

A high-speed chase. BOY on bike versus MEN in van. Inches away from death, ALEX swerves in and out of the traffic. He's almost crushed by a HUGE TRUCK that bears down on him, horn blaring. The CAMERA follows him as he crosses London, never far behind the van.

High above him, a TRAFFIC CAMERA records his process. And once again, just like in the cemetery...

A BLACK-AND-WHITE INSERT. ALEX is being watched. We see a TV MONITOR reflected in a pair of glasses. It's over in an instant.

ALEX crosses the Thames - we see the river stretching out below him. Now he's heading south...

                                    CUT TO:

28   **EXT.   SLATER'S CAR-BREAKING YARD   DAY.** 28

ALEX comes to a halt outside a huge car-breaking yard somewhere in South London. Towers of burned and broken cars. A sign reads:

> JEFF SLATER. AUTO WRECKERS.
> *Heaven for Cars*

The van stops beside a security hut. A GUARD waves it on through an open gate.

CLOSE ON ALEX - still in his funeral suit.
Watching as...

...a crane drops a car into a crushing
machine. There is a CAR-CRUSHER OPERATOR
inside a metal-and-glass cabin attached
to the machine. He presses a button. Huge
metal fingers fold in on the car, crushing it.

The CAR-CRUSHER OPERATOR presses another button. The car is ejected as metallic toothpaste.

ANOTHER ANGLE. ALEX makes his move.

The GUARD in the security hut has opened a
newspaper. ALEX sprints forward, crouching
low, then sneaks through the gate without
being seen by the GUARD. He wheels his
bicycle with him, then tucks it away behind
a broken car.

He's in. What next?

He looks around. Moves farther into the
yard - then freezes as one of the TWO MEN
from the house walks toward the security
hut. He's a tough-looking Essex boy with
attitude, the owner of the yard.

> SLATER
> (Calling) You seen Nigel?

> WORKER
> Nah.

> SLATER
> Well, if you see him, tell
> him I want him.

ALEX hurries forward, taking cover behind
another car. The crane is still at work -
a huge grappling hook, not a magnet. And
then he sees...

IAN RIDER'S CAR. Registration number:
R1D3R. Unmistakable. From this angle, it

doesn't look too badly damaged. A bit crum-
pled at the front, but otherwise OK.

ALEX looks around. Sprints over to it.
Crouches beside it. He runs a hand along
the trunk, almost affectionately, remem-
bering the man who once drove it. But
there's clearly something wrong. This car
hasn't been involved in a crash.

ALEX creeps round the side of the car. His
eyes widen in shock. He's seen the true cause
of the "accident." The driver's window is
smashed, fragments of glass still scattered
on the seats. But there's also a line of bullet holes in the paneling. ALEX reaches out
and touches them. Unbelieving. And then...
SLATER and the other man from the house -
HARRY - approach the car. ALEX hears them
before he sees them.

> SLATER
> The Rider car should have
> been done two days ago. So
> do it now. All right?

They're getting closer and closer. ALEX realizes there's nowhere to hide. Except inside
the car itself! He makes his decision. As
SLATER and HARRY appear, walking toward the
car, he opens the door and gets in.

He's just closed the door when they arrive.

> HARRY
> I didn't get the paperwork.

> SLATER
> Just do it, Harry. I'm off
> to Liverpool Street.

> HARRY
> The station.

> SLATER
> Where else, you berk. I'm
> taking them the stuff...

The two men walk away.

INSIDE THE CAR. ALEX has heard all this. He glances at the dashboard, taking in the car's expensive CD system.

FROM OUTSIDE THE CAR. The sound of a whistle. ALEX looks up, puzzled...

...just as the grappling hook from the crane plunges down, smashing into the car. The hook closes around the roof, buckling it. The sunroof shatters.

INSIDE THE CAR. Dust and metal particles rain down. ALEX realizes he has to get out fast. He tries to open the door. But the grappling iron has jammed it shut.

ALEX tries to kick the door open.

ANOTHER ANGLE. The CRANE OPERATOR jerks the lever that lifts the car off the ground.

INSIDE THE CAR. ALEX feels himself being lifted into the air. Ten feet, eleven feet, twelve... His foot smashes into the door. It won't open.

WIDER ANGLE. The car swings around and over the crusher. Then it's dumped inside it.

Inside his cabin, THE CAR-CRUSHER OPERATOR presses the first button. There is a grinding of machinery as the metal fingers of the CAR CRUSHER begin to close in.

INSIDE THE CAR. ALEX is trapped in a hideous nightmare, the metal walls closing in on the car, the car beginning to buckle and break, the very daylight being squeezed out. Glass and metal cascade around him. There's no escape. He has seconds left...

...and then the car's CD PLAYER - we saw it when IAN RIDER was being pursued - twists around. Something somewhere has short-circuited and activated it. The CD PLAYER hides a complicated, hi-tech CONTROL PANEL. A series of lights flicker into active mode. Several words appear on a miniature screen:

FRONT MISSILE LAUNCH
REAR MISSILE LAUNCH
EJECTOR SEAT

ALEX stares. What does it mean? It seems crazy. But what else can he do? The car is crumpling all around him. He makes a deci- sion, reaches out and twists the knob until EJECTOR SEAT is highlighted. Then he presses the button.

ANOTHER ANGLE. The fingers of the crusher have almost completed their work, but then there's an explosion. A burst of smoke. At the same time, ALEX is rocketed out between the fingers of the car crusher and into the air. He shoots past the grappling hook of the crane that is moving overhead.

And then catches hold of it on his way back down.

ANGLE ON CAR-CRUSHER OPERATOR. As the machine comes to a grinding halt, he won- ders what has happened and scrabbles out of the cabin.

                    OPERATOR
        What...?

BACK ON ALEX. As he lets go of the hook and drops down onto a pile of cars. He stops there, unable to believe what has just happened. Unable to believe what he just did. But this is no time to hang around.

The CARS provide him with a fast way back down to the ground. But the OPERATOR has seen him.

                    OPERATOR
        You! Come here!

As ALEX scrabbles down, the alarm is raised
and WORKERS begin to close in on him from
all sides.

> OPERATOR
>> Get him...!

ALEX reaches the ground. He runs around a
pile of cars and comes face-to-face with
SLATER and another WORKER.

> SLATER
>> All right. Hold it right
>> there.

The WORKER is holding a monkey wrench.
Holding it like a weapon. ALEX simply can't
believe this...

> ALEX
>> (To the WORKER) Wait...

The WORKER swings the monkey wrench. ALEX
ducks, then lashes out at SLATER. He's a
brilliant karate fighter and knows all the
moves. SLATER is thrown back. The WORKER
comes at ALEX again with the monkey wrench.
SLATER recovers and runs forward (behind
ALEX). The WORKER throws the monkey wrench
at ALEX. The lethal object spins through
the air. ALEX drops, acting instinctively.
The monkey wrench knocks out SLATER.

The WORKER gapes, seeing what he's done. At
the same moment, ALEX lashes out and the
WORKER goes flying.

A SECURITY CAMERA mounted high above swivels
toward him as...

...more WORKERS approach. This time a pair
of them. Two against one. More confident by
the second, ALEX takes them both out.

ALEX runs down a path defined by the wrecked
cars on either side - great towers, rising
up above him. The path ahead is suddenly
blocked by three more WORKERS running toward

him. ALEX ducks off up a second path, disappearing between two towers. At the bottom
of one of these towers, a wrecked ICE-CREAM
VAN.

The three WORKERS chase after him and disappear from sight. A beat, then the door of
the ICE-CREAM VAN opens and ALEX steps back
out onto the path he had first taken.

He pauses a moment, but then there's a shot
and the window of the ICE-CREAM VAN shatters.

More WORKERS chase toward him. ALEX runs off.

WIDER ANGLE. Not trying to hide now, ALEX
sprints through the car yard, ducking and
dodging as bullets fly into cars, ricocheting
off metal.

He finds his bike and snatches it up. Jumps
on it. Pedals. Bullets still flying.

The GUARD has been slow to react. He comes out
of the hut as ALEX rides through the gate.
ALEX lashes out with one foot, speeding past
on the bike. The foot crashes into the GUARD'S
chest. The GUARD is thrown back into the hut.

ALEX speeds down the cul-de-sac and disappears.

                                CUT TO:

29 **INT.   IAN RIDER'S HOUSE - KITCHEN   DAY.**   29

A moment when we see JACK STARBRIGHT as the
nanny she must once have been. She's seeing to a cut on ALEX'S arm. ALEX is dirty
and excited...just back from the yard.

                    ALEX
          I couldn't believe what I
          was doing. This guy just
          came at me and...

ALEX repeats the karate moves that took out

the last attacker at SLATER'S yard. JACK
applies iodine. And that cuts ALEX down to
size. He winces...like he always winced.
Even when he was a little kid.

> JACK
> That's not what those karate
> lessons were for. Don't
> forget-I was into karate too.

> ALEX
> You were into the teacher.

> JACK
> He was cute...

> ALEX
> What were they doing, Jack?
> And why were they here?

JACK meets ALEX'S eyes. She has something
to show him.

CUT TO:

30   **INT.   IAN RIDER'S HOUSE - STUDY   DAY.**   30

JACK and ALEX stand together, stunned. The
entire room has been cleared out. No respect
for IAN'S memory. Everything has been taken.
They just stand and stare at each other.

CUT TO:

31   **EXT. LIVERPOOL STREET STATION - CONCOURSE DAY.**   31

JACK and ALEX (in fresh clothes) arrive at
a long terrace overlooking the main concourse of the station.

In front of them, a huge, animated advertise-
ment on one of the station billboards.
The handsome, smiling face of DARRIUS SAYLE
with his hi-tech STORMBREAKER computer.
The head turns and he's looking straight
at CAMERA - and suddenly he's more
sinister than smiling. There's a headline:

STORMBREAKER: COMING SOON TO A SCHOOL NEAR YOU.

Finally, at the bottom, the name of the company: SAYLE ENTERPRISES.

> JACK
> You're sure they said they were coming here? They could have gone anywhere!

> ALEX
> No. They didn't say they were taking a train. They said they had to bring stuff here - to the station.

> JACK
> Where?

ALEX looks down at the concourse.

> ALEX
> Over there!

ALEX has seen JOHN CRAWFORD, making his way through the CROWD.

> JACK
> That's the guy from the funeral. That's...

JACK turns to ALEX. But before she can remember the name of the man, ALEX has already gone, down the stairs and into the main part of the concourse. Exasperated, JACK calls after him.

> JACK
> Alex...!

ANOTHER ANGLE. As ALEX pushes his way through the CROWD, trying not to lose sight of CRAWFORD.

Where is he? He's gone! ALEX is about to give up in despair, but then he sees CRAWFORD at the far end of the main concourse.

And a SECURITY CAMERA swivels to follow him.

BLACK-AND-WHITE. ALEX being watched on a monitor. Reflected in a pair of glasses. A MAN watching...

> BLUNT
> (voice only)
> He's on his way...

32   **EXT. LIVERPOOL STREET STATION - CONCOURSE DAY.**   32

BACK ON THE CONCOURSE. To one side, a PHOTO BOOTH - glowing like a space capsule. Slightly surreal. ALEX just has time to see CRAWFORD go in. There's a flash. Then two more.

A final flash. The curtain opens.

And here's the surprise. A completely different person - a LARGE WOMAN gets out! The machine spits out some photographs. The WOMAN takes the photographs and walks down the platform toward the barriers.

ANOTHER ANGLE. ALEX is totally puzzled. Slowly, he approaches the PHOTO BOOTH. He hesitates, then goes in.

> CUT TO:

33   **INT.   PHOTOGRAPH MACHINE   DAY.**   33

There's a seat, a curtain, and a camera behind a glass panel. A slot demanding a coin. Not sure he's doing the right thing, ALEX closes the curtain, then puts a coin in the slot.

A pause. The machine gears itself up. We almost hear the ticking, as if its about to explode. Then...

A FLASH.

ALEX is momentarily blinded.

A SECOND FLASH. And suddenly ALEX finds himself moving...

CUT TO:

34   **INT.   TUNNEL   DAY.**   34

The seat from the photo booth is travel-ing on rails through a tunnel. ALEX is shocked.

CUT TO:

35   **INT.   MI6 ARRIVALS HALL   DAY.**   35

The seat, with ALEX on it, arrives in a functional but still slightly futuristic room deep inside the headquarters of MI6 - Britain's top secret spy organization. ALEX swivels around.

MRS. JONES is in the room, waiting for him.

> MRS. JONES
> Good morning, Alex. Shouldn't you be at school?

ALEX looks around him, confused and more than a little nervous, trying to take this all in.

> ALEX
> (Slowly) I was on the plat-form at Liverpool Street Station. And now I'm here.

> MRS. JONES
> That's right.

> ALEX
> So what is this place?

> MRS. JONES
> Please, come with me...

She leads a disbelieving ALEX out of the room.

                              CUT TO:

36   **EXT. LIVERPOOL STREET STATION - PLATFORM DAY.**   36

No sign of ALEX. JACK is getting worried. She
walks past the PHOTO BOOTH, looking for him.

Unseen by her, four PHOTOGRAPHS spit out.
They show ALEX reacting in shock, his hair
blowing in the wind, as he is carried
through the tunnel.

                              CUT TO:

37   **INT.   MI6 ATRIUM   DAY.**   37

The atrium of a busy, modern office. Lots
of maps and computers. MEN and WOMEN
moving with a sense of purpose. ALEX follows
MRS. JONES.

                    MRS. JONES
          I think you've probably
          realized that your uncle
          didn't work for a bank. The
          Royal and General doesn't
          exist. He worked for us.

                    ALEX
          Who are you?

                    MRS. JONES
          My name is Mrs. Jones, I
          run the Special Operations
          division of MI6.

                    ALEX
          Wait a minute. You're say-
          ing he lied to me.

MRS. JONES sees ALEX's distress.

                    MRS. JONES
          I'm sorry, Alex. He lied to

everyone. It was part of
his job.

They turn a corner and disappear from
sight...

                                    CUT TO:

38   **INT.   MI6 - GALLERY   DAY.**   38

ALEX follows MRS. JONES through an open plan
area with many serious-looking OPERATIVES
working at computer consoles and desks. ALEX
has been badly stung by the truth.

                    MRS. JONES
          Ian Rider was one of our
          best agents.

                    ALEX
          Until you got him killed.

                    MRS. JONES
          He got himself killed. An
          occupational hazard.

                    ALEX
          Not if you're a banker.

MRS. JONES stops by a door. The name ALAN
BLUNT on the front.

                    MRS. JONES
          Mr. Blunt wants to talk to
          you, Alex. We have a
          proposition we'd like to
          make.

MRS. JONES opens the door for ALEX.

                                    CUT TO:

39   **INT.   BLUNT'S OFFICE   DAY.**   39

BLUNT is standing in front of what looks
like a view out of the window...Big Ben.

                    BLUNT
We want you to work for us.

                    ALEX
You're not being serious.

                    BLUNT
     Actually, it's not my habit
     to make jokes.

BLUNT sits down. The view of Big Ben is
actually a photo on the wall of his large,
executive office. There's a TV plasma
screen and a window overlooking Liverpool
Street.

                    ALEX
Well, you're making one now.

ALEX looks from BLUNT to MRS. JONES. He is
utterly cold. She avoids his eye.

                    ALEX
     I don't want to be a spy.
     In case you hadn't noticed,
     I'm still at school.

                    BLUNT
     I'll take that as a "no,"
     then. What a great shame.
     Your uncle would have been
     very disappointed.

                    ALEX
What?

                    BLUNT
     Letting him down, like
     that. But I suppose. Young
     people...

BLUNT has gone for the jugular. MRS. JONES
glances at him and we get a sense that
she's not happy with the situation.

                    ALEX
How can you say that? He

wouldn't want me to be here. He spent his whole life making sure I never knew anything about this.

> BLUNT
> Then how do you explain this?

BLUNT presses a button on his desk and the plasma screen comes to life.

ON THE SCREEN - a secret camera shows the fight at SLATER'S CAR-CRUSHING YARD. BLUNT watches as ALEX goes through his karate moves.

> BLUNT
> Downward block. Counter to reverse kick. Perfectly executed. Who trained you?

> ALEX
> Nobody trained me.

> BLUNT
> You're a first-grade *Dan*, Alex. A black belt at karate. Who paid for the lessons?

> ALEX
> It was my choice!

> BLUNT
> (Hitting the button again)
> No!

The images stop.

> BLUNT
> All your life, Ian Rider was preparing you. You speak French, German, and Japanese.

> ALEX
> He took me on holiday.

                    BLUNT
          You've been scuba diving,
          mountain climbing, abseil-
          ing...

                    ALEX
          They were hobbies...

                    BLUNT
          White-water rafting, mar-
          tial arts. He was training
          you...

                    ALEX
          (Interrupting) No! You're
          trying to spoil every-
          thing, but that's not how
          it was.

                    BLUNT
          ...and rifle shooting.

BLUNT produces a paper target. One of
ALEX's. All the bullet holes are grouped
around the bull's-eye.

ALEX stands up. These people are undermin-
ing everything he's ever believed in. And
he's made up his mind.

                    ALEX
          I don't care what you say. I'm
          not interested. Now, can you
          put me back in the photo booth
          and show me the way out.

MRS. JONES is almost pleased.

                    MRS. JONES
          I'll take him.

                    BLUNT
          No. Let me.

A miniature war fought over possession of
ALEX RIDER.

CUT TO:

40   **INT.   MI6 - ARRIVALS HALL   DAY.**   40

BLUNT and ALEX approach the PHOTO BOOTH a
second time. They arrive just as an OPER-
ATIVE gets into the seat.

>   BLUNT
>   I'm surprised, really. I'd
>   have thought you'd want to
>   get back at the people who
>   killed your uncle.

Contemptuous silence from ALEX. The OPER-
ATIVE is spun through the wall.

>   BLUNT
>   How is that housekeeper of
>   yours, by the way? What's
>   her name? Jack Starbright. I
>   suppose she'll have started
>   packing by now.

>   ALEX
>   Why? What do you mean?

>   BLUNT
>   Didn't she tell you? Her
>   visa ran out seven years
>   ago. She'll be deported any
>   day now. Actually, we might
>   decide to prosecute her
>   first. Make an example...

An empty seat has arrived back. But ALEX
doesn't sit down. He's staring at BLUNT.

>   ALEX
>   (Revolted) What are you...?
>   What sort of people are you?

>   BLUNT
>   Ones who normally get their way.

BLUNT smiles, knowing he's won.

CUT TO:

41   **EXT.   TRAINING CAMP   DAY.**   41

ESTABLISHING SHOT. A series of wooden barracks and a truly murderous assault course
set in a hostile landscape - the Brecon
Beacons, a mountain range somewhere in
Wales.

Special forces SOLDIERS run past carrying
huge logs strapped to their wrists. ALEX,
also dressed in combats, walks with a
tough-looking SERGEANT. Taking this all
in. Not exactly happy to be here.

            SOLDIERS
    (Singing) You heard what
    the sergeant said. Drop
    that log you'll wish you're
    dead. We don't like this,
    we're in pain. And so we'll
    do it all again.

More SOLDIERS running with heavy rucksacks
and full battle dress. Another SOLDIER
sliding down a diagonal wire over a swamp.

The two of them reach a wooden barracks and
go in.

CUT TO:

42   **INT.   K UNIT - BARRACKS   DAY.**   42

Four men, all in their twenties, as tough
as they come.

They only have code names: WOLF, FOX,
EAGLE (the youngest), and BEAR. Two are
resting. One is cleaning an automatic pistol. The last is reading a paperback book.
WOLF is their leader. Handsome and cold-
blooded.

The SERGEANT comes into the room. ALEX is
with him, carrying his kit bag.

                    SERGEANT
          On your feet!

Everyone springs to attention.

                    SERGEANT
          Gentlemen. This is our lat-
          est recruit. He's here for
          two weeks' training. Don't
          ask me about it because I
          don't know a thing! I just
          do what I'm told. (To ALEX)
          We have no names here. We
          have no ranks. This is K
          Unit. Fox. Bear. Eagle. And
          Wolf. You'll be Cub.

The SERGEANT glances at the men.

                    SERGEANT
          Get him a bed.

The SERGEANT turns and leaves.

ALEX is on his own with these extremely
tough men. He's about as welcome as a cock-
roach. For a moment no one speaks. Then
they uncoil slowly...

                    FOX
          What the...

                    BEAR
          Jesus!

WOLF comes over to ALEX. Totally unfriendly.

                    WOLF
          Who the hell do you think
          you are? A schoolboy!

                    FOX
          They've got to be joking.

                    WOLF
          What's your name? Who sent
          you here?

                    ALEX
       I can't tell you.

                    WOLF
      You can't tell me?

Suddenly WOLF lashes out and grabs hold of
ALEX around the neck. ALEX winces but tries
not to show any pain.

                    WOLF
      You can tell me.

                    ALEX
      No...

WOLF tightens his grip. The other MEN watch
uneasily.

                    WOLF
      You with Special Operations?
      They're the only ones daft
      enough to come up with some-
      thing like this.

                    ALEX
      I said...

ALEX performs an amazing countermove, twisting around and slamming a foot into WOLF'S
stomach. WOLF lets go and falls back, winded.

The other MEN are impressed, but they're
not going to show it in front of WOLF.

                    ALEX
      ...I can't tell you.

                    WOLF
      (Gasping) Someone been teaching
      you self-defense? Well, that's
      not going to help you here.

WOLF gets to his feet.

                    WOLF
      You won't last two days...

CUT TO:

43 **EXT.   CEMETERY - IAN RIDER'S GRAVE   DAY.** 43

JACK STARBRIGHT is laying flowers on IAN'S grave. She senses movement behind her and turns to see MRS. JONES waiting to speak to her.

CUT TO:

44 **EXT.   CEMETERY   DAY.**   44

JACK and MRS. JONES walk together in another part of the cemetery.

> JACK
> I don't believe this. I don't believe any of it. (Beat) Where is he now?

> MRS. JONES
> We can't tell you that. I'm sorry.

> JACK
> (Scornful) You're sorry? What are you sorry about? Taking him out of school? Trying to turn him into something... (Beat) Alex isn't a spy! He's fourteen years old, for heaven's sake.

> MRS. JONES
> (Forcing herself to be cold) That's what makes him useful to us.

> JACK
> And what happens if he gets hurt? What if he's killed? Could you live with that?

MRS. JONES can't answer. But we can see that she too is worried about ALEX.

                    JACK
          I worked with Ian Rider for
          nine years. Nine years and
          I never knew anything about
          all this. But I'm warning
          you, Mrs. Jones. If any-
          thing happens to Alex...

                    MRS. JONES
          (Interrupting) It won't.
          We'll look after him. I
          promise you. (Beat) By the
          way, he asked me to give
          you this.

MRS. JONES hands JACK an envelope. JACK is
puzzled.

                    MRS. JONES
          Your visa. It's permanent.

MRS. JONES walks away. And suddenly JACK
understands the price ALEX has paid.

                              CUT TO:

45   **EXT.   BRECON BEACONS - HILLSIDE   DAY.**   45

TRAINING MONTAGE BEGINS.

WOLF, EAGLE, FOX, and BEAR run past with
heavy rucksacks: full kit, combat boots,
etc. Other SOLDIERS are also running.

ALEX has a slightly smaller pack than the
others. But he still struggles to keep up.

                              CUT TO:

46   **EXT.   BRECON BEACONS - RIVER   DAY.**   46

ALEX follows WOLF, FOX, EAGLE, BEAR, and
other SOLDIERS over a deep river. The water
rises up to the men's chests and they hold
their rifles above their heads. We hear them
singing:

                    SOLDIERS
          (Singing) Keep that gun
          above your head...

The water rises right over ALEX. Only his
rifle, held up, is visible as he crosses
the water. We hear him gurgling the song
underwater.

                              CUT TO:

47 **EXT. BRECON BEACONS - ASSAULT COURSE   DAY.** 47

WOLF, FOX, EAGLE, and BEAR climb a net and
throw themselves over the other side. ALEX
is quite a bit behind. The SERGEANT is on
the other side, unimpressed.

                    SERGEANT
          (Shouting) You're not in
          the playground now, Cub!
          Move it!

ALEX grits his teeth and throws himself
over the top.

                              CUT TO:

48 **EXT.   BRECON BEACONS - ROPEWALK   DAY**   48

ANOTHER ANGLE. ALEX on a tree walk...two
ropes suspended high in the air. He reaches
the end - a platform, the SERGEANT waiting
there, a rope slanting down diagonally to the
ground. The SOLDIERS shoot down at great
speed, unhook themselves, and run.

WOLF waits for ALEX, who hooks himself to
the rope, gathering his strength to make
the jump. But before he is ready.

                    WOLF
          Let me give you a hand, Cub.

WOLF pushes ALEX into the air. ALEX shoots
down, out of control. There's a slimy,

muddy pool at the bottom and ALEX is dragged right through it. Dripping mud from head to toe.

ALEX doesn't move. FOX, EAGLE, and BEAR are laughing at him. WOLF too.

CLOSE ON ALEX. A pivotal moment. Dripping wet, exhausted, on his own...he's almost ready to break down, almost ready to pack the whole thing in.

But he's not going to. Grimly, determinedly, he gets to his feet.

                                    CUT TO:

49   **EXT.   BRECON BEACONS - FIELD   NIGHT.**   49

ALEX, WOLF, FOX, EAGLE, and BEAR are slithering across a field on their stomachs. Full camouflage. Faces blackened. A lot of tension. They're somewhere dangerous.

WOLF raises a hand to stop everyone. He takes out a map and examines it with a flashlight, shielding it with a hand.

ANOTHER ANGLE. A huge searchlight flashes on. More SOLDIERS - rise up all around them, machine guns raised. They're surrounded.

                    SOLDIER
          (Taunting) Well, well, well.
          What have we got here?

ON WOLF. His face is filled with fury.

TRAINING MONTAGE ENDS.

                                    CUT TO:

50   **EXT.   SOLDIERS' CAMP   DAWN.**   50

ESTABLISHING SHOT. An abandoned farmyard, somewhere in the Brecon Beacons. A few brick buildings, most of them derelict.

A few ARMY TRUCKS parked in the distance.
Also, on a slight slope, an S-250 GRASS
SHELTER. It's basic army issue - the **G**ichner
Relocatable **A**ccommodations **S**helter **S**ystem
is essentially a large, ungainly portakabin
perched high up on wheels.

Two SOLDIERS are sliding the bolts across
the metal door of a small cottage with a
chimney and barred window.

>   SOLDIER
> Au revoir, boys!

>   SOLDIER (2)
> Special forces today. Catering
> corps tomorrow.

The two of them laugh. One of them stays
on guard duty. The other begins walking
toward the GRASS SHELTER.

>   CUT TO:

51   **INT.   ABANDONED COTTAGE   DAWN.**   51

FOX kicks out at the locked door of
the cottage. The interior is bare, the
ceiling missing between the two
floors. There's the barred window but
nothing else. EAGLE and BEAR are with
him. WOLF is standing on his own on an
upper level. ALEX meanwhile seems to
be pacing the length of the room,
checking the wall.

>   FOX
> We're finished! We blew
> the whole exercise - we'll
> get binned.

He suddenly turns on WOLF, jabbing an accu-
satory finger.

>   FOX
> This is your fault! You had
> the map...!

WOLF says nothing. FOX is right.

ANOTHER ANGLE. ALEX has found what he was looking for. A certain spot on the wall. WOLF notices him.

ALEX lashes out - a karate kick. His foot goes straight through the wall. Everyone turns to look at him.

>   ALEX
>   There's a fireplace.

>   FOX
>   How did you know?

>   ALEX
>   I saw the chimney on the way in.

ALEX - helped now by EAGLE - prises away the broken panel to reveal a large fire-place. Dust and soot come rushing down.

>   EAGLE
>   The kid's right. It's clear.

>   BEAR
>   Sure. You think they'd just
>   leave it if they thought we
>   could all climb up?

>   ALEX
>   You can't. You're too big.

A pause. FOX turns to WOLF. And like it or not, they both know ALEX is right.

A FEW MOMENTS LATER...

FOX and EAGLE are in the fireplace, lifting ALEX up. They push. ALEX disappears from sight.

>   CUT TO:

52   **EXT.   SOLDIERS' CAMP   DAWN.**   52

ALEX climbs out of the chimney and squats

low on the roof, looking around him. The
soot will make good camouflage.

The SOLDIER is still on guard outside the
cottage. A second SOLDIER walks over to him
from the GRASS SHELTER, carrying a steam-
ing mug of tea.

ALEX shifts his weight and to his horror
he dislodges a pebble. He watches it run
down the roof. The pebble stops briefly at
a guttering. Is everything going to be all
right? No...

> SOLDIER (2)
> We should have taken this
> lot back to base.

> SOLDIER
> Later's fine.

...the pebble falls off the roof. But luck
is with ALEX. The pebble lands unnoticed
in the mug of tea.

> SOLDIER
> Brew?

He hands the tea (and the pebble) to the
SOLDIER on duty.

> SOLDIER (2)
> Ta.

The first SOLDIER moves in the direction
of the GRASS SHELTER.

ALEX heaves a sign of relief. He scrabbles
around the back of the chimney and climbs
down a drainpipe to ground level...

...then around the front of the house. The
SOLDIER is still standing there with his mug
of tea.

ON ALEX. Wondering what to do. He notices
the GRASS SHELTER. And has an idea.

CUT TO:

53   **EXT.   SOLDIERS' CAMP   DAWN.**   53

ALEX stealthily approaches the GRASS SHELTER.

>   SOLDIER (3)
>   (voice-over)
>   What's happening?

>   SOLDIER
>   (voice-over)
>   (Sneering) Nothing.

>   SOLDIER (3)
>   (voice-over)
>   (Contemptuous) Bunch of losers.

The wheels have got chocks to stop
them rolling. He pulls the chocks away,
then slips around the back of the GRASS
SHELTER.

ALEX freezes as another SOLDIER walks past.

>   SOLDIER
>   (voice-over)
>   Why did they have a kid
>   with them?

>   SOLDIER (4)
>   (voice-over)
>   I don't know...

>   SOLDIER
>   (voice-over)
>   Fourteen. Bit young for the
>   Special Forces.

ALEX releases the brake at the back of the
GRASS SHELTER, presses his shoulder to the
side, and begins to push.

>   SOLDIER (3)
>   (voice-over)
>   Boss...

>   SOLDIER
>   (voice-over)
>   Yeah? What is it?

A beat.

>   SOLDIER (3)
>   (voice-over)
>   Are we moving?

>   CUT TO:

54   **EXT.   SOLDIERS' CAMP   DAWN.**   54

The slope has gotten steeper and the GRASS
SHELTER is moving fast now, away from the
farm and down a hillside. ALEX steps back,
watching it go.

ANOTHER ANGLE. The SOLDIER outside the
cottage has seen it too.

>   SOLDIER (2)
>   Hey...!

The SOLDIER runs off in pursuit of the
speeding GRASS SHELTER. Behind him, WOLF
and the other SPECIAL FORCES MEN see what
is happening through the window.

Other SOLDIERS also appear from the fringes of
the camp and chase the shelter down the hill.

>   CUT TO:

55   **INT.   GRASS SHELTER   DAWN.**   55

The six SOLDIERS try to scramble for the
door. Beginning to panic.

>   CUT TO:

56   **EXT.   SOLDIERS' CAMP   DAWN.**   56

ALEX opens the door for WOLF, EAGLE, BEAR, and
FOX. They come out into the empty farm compound.

                    EAGLE
        Where is everyone?

                    ALEX
        They sloped off.

WOLF comes out of the building and sees
what has happened. He meets ALEX's eyes.

                              CUT TO:

57 **EXT.   HILLSIDE   DAWN.**   57

The GRASS SHELTER - now moving at high
speed - continues its journey down the
hillside. And the surprise...

The hillside suddenly stops. There's a one-
hundred-foot drop with a lake at the bottom.
The GRASS SHELTER - very small in the great
landscape - shoots like a rocket into the
air. But before it reaches the water, we...

                              CUT TO:

58 **INT.   BLUNT'S OFFICE   DAY.**   58

SPLASH! ALAN BLUNT drops a lump of sugar into
a cup of tea.

It's the following morning. A uniformed
MAJOR confronts an impassive BLUNT and MRS.
JONES.

                    MAJOR
        Cuts. Bruises. Fractured
        limbs. It's just a miracle
        no one was killed.

                    BLUNT
        I'm very sorry, Major. We
        will be talking to our man.
        (Beat) Boy.

The MAJOR turns and leaves. He pauses by
the door.

                    MAJOR
          He's not a child. He's a
          lethal weapon.

He goes. BLUNT turns to MRS. JONES.

                    BLUNT
          He's ready.

But MRS. JONES is unhappy. She's not so
sure.

                              CUT TO:

59 **EXT.   K UNIT - BARRACKS   DAY.**   59

ALEX is on his own, heaving his kit bag
onto the back of a waiting jeep. It's time
to go. He's sad ... being ignored even now.
But then there's a movement behind him.
ALEX turns to see WOLF. And for once WOLF
is uneasy.

                    WOLF
          I heard you're leaving.

                    ALEX
          That's right. Yeah.

A pause. ALEX isn't expecting any kindness.

                    WOLF
          What you did last night...
          If it wasn't for you...

A pause. Then WOLF takes off his cap badge.
From the way he holds it, we know it means
a lot to him.

                    WOLF
          Here.

ALEX takes it. He meets WOLF'S eyes and
sees the respect. WOLF turns and leaves. A
new friendship has begun.

                                        CUT TO:

60   **NEWS REPORT**   60

     INT.   NEWS STUDIO   DAY.

     News Anchor speaks directly to CAMERA.

                    NEWS ANCHOR
               And finally, the most gen-
               erous gift ever made to the
               British nation.

61   **ADVERTISING PROMO**   61

     Shots of the Stormbreaker, an amazingly
     designed computer.

                    NEWS ANCHOR
                    (voice-over)
               The Stormbreaker has been
               called the most sophisti-
               cated personal computer
               of the 21st century...

62   **NEWSPAPER FRONT PAGES**   62

     Photographs of DARRIUS SAYLE and head-
     lines. SAYLE OF THE CENTURY. THE
     COMPUTER KING. FREE STORMBREAKER FOR
     EVERY SCHOOL.

                    NEWS ANCHOR
                    (voice-over)
               ...and one month ago, its
               multibillionaire inventor,
               Darrius Sayle, made his
               astonishing announcement.

                                        CUT TO:

63   **EXT.   STEPS OF THE SAYLE TOWER - DAY.**   63

     Our first real sighting of DARRIUS
     SAYLE. Rakish, charming, dangerous.
     Always fastidiously dressed. He's being

interviewed on the steps of his office
building by news reporter VIVIEN CREEGOR.

>   SAYLE
> That's right, Vivien. I want
> to give a free Stormbreaker
> to every school in the coun-
> try. And while I'm at it,
> I wouldn't mind giving you
> one too.

>   VIVIEN CREEGOR
> (Blushing) Really, Mr Sayle!

                                CUT TO:

64 **INT.   NEWS STUDIO   DAY.**   64

>   NEWS ANCHOR
> The PM has given his full
> support   to Mr. Sayle...

                                CUT TO:

65 **INT.   PRESS ROOM   DAY.**   65

The PRIME MINISTER announces the news.

>   PRIME MINISTER
> This is a wonderful oppor-
> tunity for British schools
> and I'm very happy to say
> that Mr. Sayle has asked me
> to press the button that
> will bring all the computers
> online.

66 **FRONT COVER - *FORTUNE* MAGAZINE**   66

A powerful photograph of a powerful man. A
headline: INSIDE DARRIUS SAYLE...

>   NEWS ANCHOR
> The prime minister and
> Darrius Sayle have already
> met. It turns out that they

were at school together. This
little-known fact emerged
recently...

A hand reaches forward and presses a remote
control, freezing the image.

                                        CUT TO:

67 **INT.   MI6 - BLUNT'S OFFICE   DAY.**   67

ALEX is back with BLUNT and MRS. JONES.

                    BLUNT
        We don't trust him.

                    ALEX
        Why not?

                    BLUNT
        Well, we don't trust anyone.
        It's sort of what we're for.

                  MRS. JONES
        We always thought that
        Darrius Sayle was too good
        to be true.

                    BLUNT
        So six months ago we put an
        agent in to keep an eye on him.

                    ALEX
        You're talking about my uncle.

                    BLUNT
        Yes. (Beat) Sayle has a
        manufacturing plant in
        Cornwall. Built on top of
        what used to be a tin mine.
        Ian Rider went there as a
        security guard.

                  MRS. JONES
        And he found something. In
        his last message to us, he
        mentioned a virus.

> ALEX
> A computer virus...?

> MRS. JONES
> He was on his way to tell
> us. But he never arrived.

> BLUNT
> Something's going on. We
> need to get someone in
> there to take a look around
> and this may be our last
> chance...

> ALEX
> Why me?

> BLUNT
> I'll show you.

BLUNT brings up another image on the screen: a gangly teenager. KEVIN BLAKE. A typical computer nerd. He's made the front cover of *DISC DRIVE WORLD*. A starburst reads: COMPETITION WINNER.

> BLUNT
> This is Kevin Blake. He's
> a computer nerd. Six weeks
> ago he won a competition
> in a computer magazine.
> *Disc Drive World*. You ever
> read it?

A look from ALEX. Of course not.

> MRS. JONES
> The first prize was a visit
> to Cornwall and a chance to
> try out the Stormbreaker.
> He's due to arrive tomorrow.

> BLUNT
> It's a PR stunt. I imagine
> Mr. Sayle was trying to
> show the world what a nice
> man he was. Get a kiddie

in to see the works. Now
you'll take his place.

                    ALEX
But I'm nothing like him.

                    MRS. JONES
We've spoken to the editor.

MRS. JONES presses the remote control
and the magazine cover is replaced by a
second cover that is identical - except
that it now shows ALEX'S face. ALEX is
impressed. These people think of everything. But...

                    ALEX
There's just one problem...
I don't know anything about
computers. I'm not a com-
puter nerd.

                    BLUNT
But you soon will be.

BLUNT slides a dauntingly large pile of
computer books and magazines across the
desk.

                    BLUNT
We only have three days
left. There's a launch at
the Science Museum next
Friday. 70,000 Stormbreaker
computers going live...

                    MRS. JONES
We don't want you to get
into any trouble, Alex. Just
take a look around. And be
careful of Sayle. He may
seem charming.

                    BLUNT
But he's about as charming
as a snake.

                    MRS. JONES
          Keep your eyes open and
          report back.

                    ALEX
          How am I meant to do that?

                    BLUNT
          We'll supply you with a
          telecommunications device.
          That and other gadgets.

                    ALEX
          (Pleased) I get gadgets?

                                        CUT TO:

68 **EXT.   HAMLEY'S TOY SHOP   DAY.**   68

     ALEX crosses Regent Street and enters the
     world-famous toy shop. In the foreground,
     a NEWSPAPER VENDOR is selling the evening
     paper. SAYLE LAUNCHES THE STORMBREAKER
     is the headline. Another picture of the
     man...

                                        CUT TO:

69 **INT.   HAMLEY'S TOY SHOP   DAY.**   69

     A man in a three-piece suit is demonstrat-
     ing a robot dog to a rotund, spoiled BOY.
     The BOY is cradling an expensive metal car.
     His name is SMITHERS and he's barely able
     to conceal his dislike. A sign reads:
     ROBOPETS. The man is wearing a Hamley's
     name badge: SMITHERS.

                    SMITHERS
          If you pat his head, his
          tail wags. He also obeys
          certain voice commands.
          (To the dog) Roll over!

     The robot dog topples clumsily onto its
     back, its legs in the air.

> SMITHERS
> Delightful, don't you think?
> We also have robot cats and
> robot rodents!

> BOY
> I want one!

> SMITHERS
> Of course you do. Here you are.

He hands the dog to the BOY. At the same
time, ALEX approaches.

> SMITHERS
> Good morning. Can I interest
> you in a Robopet?

> ALEX
> No. I'm looking for some-
> thing to take to Cornwall.

At once SMITHERS changes. The word *Cornwall*
was what he was waiting for.

> SMITHERS
> Ah. Cornwall, yes. Come
> with me...

SMITHERS leads ALEX through a door.

>   CUT TO:

70 **INT.   HAMLEY'S - BASEMENT STOREROOM   DAY.** 70

SMITHERS leads ALEX downstairs to a private
basement.

> SMITHERS
> I keep my special toys down
> here. Somewhere children
> aren't allowed, I'm rather
> pleased to say...

They arrive in a more private area. There's
an expensive MODEL CAR to one side.

SMITHERS
Here we are. Let's start
with this...

SMITHERS produces a YO-YO.

ALEX
That's a little old-fashioned.

SMITHERS
On the contrary. It's
state-of-the-art.

SMITHERS touches the YO-YO and it irises
open electronically in his hands to reveal
a futuristic MINIATURIZED ENGINE.

SMITHERS
A miniaturized engine
with traction power up
to ninety pounds. The
main body is magnetic and
the cord is a specially
developed form of super-
nylon. It comes with bat-
teries included and a
year's guarantee.

SMITHERS produces a backpack.

SMITHERS
Here's something to put it
in.

ALEX
Right.

ALEX starts to unzip the main zip.

SMITHERS
Not that zip! You'll deploy
the parachute! Now - this
is something I'm sure will
be perfect for you.

SMITHERS takes out a tube of ointment,

marked ZIT-CLEAN: FOR HEALTHIER SKIN. He
lays it on the counter in front of him.

> ALEX
> Zit cream?

> SMITHERS
> (Demonstrating) Smear a little
> on your finger and it's
> harmless, but then apply it
> to anything metallic...

SMITHERS nonchalantly reaches out and wipes
some of the ointment onto the EXPENSIVE
MODEL CAR. A sudden metallic hiss. The CAR
dissolves - as if in a miniature road accident.

> ALEX
> (Impressed) Sweet.

> SMITHERS
> It'll work its way through
> up to eight inches of steel.

SMITHERS takes out a PEN.

> SMITHERS
> Fountain pen. Not used by
> many young people these
> days, alas. However... The
> nib can be fired from a
> range of six meters and the
> ink is sodium pentathol.
> Whoever you hit will do
> exactly what you tell them
> for the next six hours.

He hands ALEX the pen.

> SMITHERS
> But I've saved the best till
> last...

He reaches under the counter and takes out
a Nintendo DS.

> SMITHERS
> A games system. But it's been
> modified. What it does
> depends on the cartridge that
> you place in it. Slip in this
> game here - "Call-up" - and
> it's a PDA scanner and trans-
> mitter. That's how you keep
> in touch with us. "Panic
> Station" is a bug finder and
> sonic intensifier. You can
> hear a conversation two rooms
> away.

The third cartridge is called GREEN
SCREEN.

> SMITHERS
> This one turns the whole
> thing into a smoke bomb -
> with a five-second fuse.

ALEX notices the fourth cartridge.

> ALEX
> What about "Mario Kart"?

> SMITHERS
> That's just a game. I
> thought you might like it
> for the flight.

                              CUT TO:

71 **INT. IAN RIDER'S HOUSE - STAIRS/KITCHEN DAY.** 71

ALEX comes down the stairs carrying a suitcase
and the backpack. JACK STARBRIGHT is with him.

> JACK
> It's outrageous. I mean,
> even the CIA wouldn't come
> up with something like this.
> (Beat) What am I saying?
> Of course they would. (Beat)
> But it's out of the question,

Alex. You're not going. I
know what Ian would say...

                    ALEX
It was his idea.

That stops her short. A pause.

                    ALEX
He lied to me, Jack. All my life
he was preparing me for this.
Everything he ever did...he
was just manipulating me.

                    JACK
You don't know that, Alex. He
never said anything. Maybe he
was trying to protect you.

                    ALEX
(Sad) No. He knew.

JACK hesitates, then takes a postcard from
a pile of letters on the kitchen table.

                    JACK
I didn't know whether to
show you this or not. It
came while you were away.

She hands the card over to ALEX.

                    JACK
It's from Ian. He must have
posted it before...

                    ALEX
(Reading) Wish you were
here with me. There's so
much to see...

He turns the card over and we see the picture. A ruined brick construction on a hillside - in fact, the entrance to a tin mine.

                    ALEX
It's from Cornwall.

                    JACK
          He didn't mean you to go
          there now, Alex. That's
          not what he meant.

A pause. ALEX puts the card down.

                    ALEX
          It's only a few days, Jack.
          I'll be careful.

                    JACK
          You really promise me?

                    ALEX
          I promise.

                    JACK
          And Alex...

                    ALEX
          What?

JACK produces a toothbrush.

                    ALEX
          A gadget?

                    JACK
          No. It's a toothbrush.

She looks at him as if to remind him that
she was once his nanny. He takes it and they
hug.

                              CUT TO:

72 **EXT.   AIRPORT - RUNWAY   DAY.**   72

A plane touches down.

                              CUT TO:

73 **INT.   AIRPORT - ARRIVALS   DAY.**   73

A pair of sliding doors open. PASSENGERS
come through them and among them we see

ALEX, accompanied by MRS. JONES. ALEX carries his suitcase and the backpack that SMITHERS gave him.

ANOTHER ANGLE. NADIA VOLE is waiting for them. A uniquely unattractive, severe, blond-haired PR agent from Berlin. Even when she's trying to smile, she radiates hatred.

> MRS. JONES
> Mrs. Vole? I'm the editor
> of *Disc Drive World*.

> VOLE
> (Uninterested in her) Then
> this must be Kevin.

> ALEX
> That's me.

> VOLE
> You should say good-bye now.

MRS. JONES turns to face ALEX.

> MRS. JONES
> Good-bye, Kevin. I hope you find
> your stay very informative.

> ALEX
> I'm sure it will be.

ALEX leaves with NADIA VOLE. MRS JONES watches them, full of misgivings.

                              CUT TO:

74   **INT/EXT.   HUMMER/PORT TALLON   DAY.**   74

The HUMMER drives through the fishing village. The sign - PORT TALLON WELCOMES CAREFUL DRIVERS - has been glued back together.

> VOLE
> I am Nadia Vole. I work for

Mr. Sayle. Press and public
relations.

                    ALEX
PR.

                    VOLE
Yes. This is Port Tallon.
It's a fishing village.

                    ALEX
Nice place.

                    VOLE
Not if you're a fish.

                              CUT TO:

75   **INT/EXT.   CAR/CORNISH COUNTRYSIDE   DAY.** 75

Outside Port Tallon, the HUMMER drives
through beautiful Cornish countryside.
ALEX notices the ruins of an old tin
mine. There's a brick ventilation shaft
poking out of the ground and ALEX recognizes it. It was on the card that IAN
RIDER sent him.

ALEX'S cell phone bleeps. He's received
a text message. He takes it out and looks
at the screen.

TAKE CARE. JACK. XXX

IN THE DRIVING MIRROR. NADIA VOLE notices
the cell phone.

                              CUT TO:

76   **EXT.   SAYLE ENTERPRISES - CHECKPOINT   DAY.** 76

They drive past a heavily guarded checkpoint.
ALEX sees ARMED GUARDS on patrol. More PER-
SONNEL speeding back and forth on QUAD BIKES.
A landing strip for cargo planes and heli-
copters, trucks and jeeps. Laboratories and

storage depots. ALEX looks out with unease.
What has he got himself into.

>   VOLE
> Mr. Sayle has arrived.
> He'll see you immediately
> for lunch.

CUT TO:

77   **EXT.   SAYLE'S HOUSE   DAY.**   77

An extraordinary version of WINDSOR CASTLE
built for a technocrat and reimagined in
huge glass panels, gleaming steel and
brick. It's set on an island, reached by a
causeway. The HUMMER approaches.

CUT TO:

78   **INT.   SAYLE'S HOUSE - MAIN ROOM   DAY.**   78

ALEX stands in cathedral-like room with a
vast table, chairs, archways, etc. A full-
size SNOOKER TABLE to one side. The room
is dominated by a collection of HARPOONS.
STUFFED ANIMALS on the walls. And a giant
FISH TANK, built into a wall. ALEX clocks
the HARPOONS.

Then he goes over to the tank. There are no
fish in the water. The tank is occupied
only by a giant JELLYFISH, floating, evil,
silent.

>   SAYLE
>   (voice-over)
> Hey - how are you?

And at last DARRIUS SAYLE appears, walking through a majestic archway, and we
see him in the flesh. He is a man with
a presence. Confident, extremely rich,
smiling genially. He takes a lot of care
how he looks...expensive suit, smart
tie, etc.

                    SAYLE
        It's pretty cool, wouldn't
        you say?
                    ALEX
        (Hesitant) I'm not sure
        I'd want one as a pet.

                    SAYLE
        Physalia physalia. The
        Portuguese man-of-war. I
        came upon this one in the
        South China Sea. Killing
        rare animals is one of my
        hobbies. But not this one.
        This one I had to keep. You
        see, it reminds me of
        myself.

                    ALEX
        It's ninety-nine percent
        water. It has no brains.
        And no anus.

SAYLE looks at ALEX as if seeing him for
the first time. He seems completely unof-
fended.

                    SAYLE
        I think I'm going to like
        you. Excuse me...

SAYLE smiles briefly and plucks a speck of
dust off ALEX'S sleeve. A silver-blue BAR-
RACUDA with razorlike teeth swims past the
JELLYFISH. ALEX notices it.

                    SAYLE
        But that's not what I meant.
        You see, it's an outsider.
        It's silent and yet it demands
        respect. Take a look at the
        tentacles. They are covered in
        nematocysts. Stinging cells.
        If you came into contact with
        them, you'd die a very mem-
        orable death.

> ALEX
> I'm too young to die.

> SAYLE
> No, no, no. I wouldn't believe
> that. You're never too young
> to die.

NADIA VOLE appears with a wireless telephone.

> SAYLE
> Hiya, cuddles.

> VOLE
> Mr. Sayle. You have the American
> ambassador on line one.

DARRIUS SAYLE takes the phone. At the same
time, ALEX hears a strange sound from the
tank...almost like an electric shock. He
turns around.

A complete BARRACUDA SKELETON hovers in
front of the JELLYFISH and gently sinks to
the bottom. Now ALEX knows just how deadly
those nematocysts are!

> SAYLE
> (To ALEX) It seems I'm not
> going to be able to join
> you for lunch, after all,
> but I hope you'll have
> dinner with me tonight.

SAYLE rings a bell.

> SAYLE
> It's been quite a while since
> I found myself face-to-face
> with a British schoolkid. I
> can't wait to hear what you
> think of the Stormbreaker.

A door opens. A figure walks in.

Meet MR. GRIN. Not that you'd want to. Tall and
thin, dressed as a butler, MR. GRIN is very seri-

ously deformed, with hideous scars that go all
the way from the sides of his mouth to his ears.

> SAYLE
> This is Mr. Grin. My personal
> assistant.

> ALEX
> He seems to have cut him-
> self shaving...

> SAYLE
> That's funny! (beat) Mr.
> Grin used to work in a cir-
> cus. It was a novelty knife-
> throwing act. For a climax,
> he used to catch a spinning
> knife between his teeth.

> ALEX
> And?

> SAYLE
> His mother waved to him from
> the front row and he made a
> mistake with his timing.

> MR. GRIN
> Urgh.

> SAYLE
> Mr. Grin can't talk. He'll
> show you to your room and
> we'll meet again tonight. OK?

ALEX leaves. SAYLE watches him with a hint
of suspicion.

> SAYLE
> Have fun!

> CUT TO:

79   **INT.   SAYLE'S HOUSE - ALEX'S ROOM   DAY.**   79

ALEX stands in a cavernous and well-
appointed room. His cases are on the bed.

He goes over to the window and looks out.
A patrol of four ARMED GUARDS marches past
on the lawn.

He goes to his case and takes out the NINTENDO
DS. He slots in "Panic Station." The screen
of the NINTENDO DS shows radar lines and the
machine begins to bleep.

ALEX sweeps the room. The lines converge and
the bleeping gets faster as he arrives at a
circular disk that is part of the molding
on the wall. ALEX flicks it - hard - with
his finger.

                                    CUT TO:

80   **INT.   SAYLE'S HOUSE - SECRET RADIO ROOM**   80

NADIA VOLE is wearing headphones and
plugged into a radio receiver. She reels
backward and almost falls off her chair as
there's a screech of feedback from the bug.

                                    CUT TO:

81   **INT.   SAYLE'S HOUSE - ALEX'S ROOM   DAY.**   81

A knock at the door. ALEX opens it. NADIA
VOLE is standing there. She has cotton-wool
pads in her ears.

                    VOLE
          Are you settled in, Kevin?
          It is time for you to see
          the Stormbreaker.

                                    CUT TO:

82   **INT.   SAYLE ENTERPRISES - CHAMBER   DAY.**   82

ALEX enters a truly futuristic, hi-tech chamber. There is a central platform. Various
pieces of electronic equipment, including
several monitors. NADIA VOLE is with him.

                    VOLE
          You are the first child to
          experience the power, the
          world domination, of the
          Stormbreaker. This model
          has been already loaded
          with highly developed pro-
          grams for all aspects of
          the school curriculum.

                    ALEX
          (Deliberately goading her)
          Does it have pinball?

ALEX steps onto the platform.

                    VOLE
          Be still, please, while we
          scan you.

VOLE presses the controls and various CAM-
ERAS and LASER SCANNERS swivel over ALEX
and begin measuring his body. He is being
filmed from head to toe.

                    ALEX
          You're using slice-matrix
          virtual-reality software.

                    VOLE
          (Impressed) Yes! Who taught
          you about computers, Kevin?

                    ALEX
          My uncle.

                    VOLE
          He was a computer whiz-king?

                    ALEX
          No. He was a security guard.
          But he died.

                    VOLE
          How did that happen?

                    ALEX
          I don't know. But one day
          I'll find out.

                    VOLE
          Maybe. But not today.

She presses a button. The scanning finishes.
On the outer monitors, a MATRIX image of ALEX
comes together and rotates 360 degrees. Text
information - age, weight, hair color, eye
color, etc. - scrolls upward. A screen
flashes: PROGRAMMING COMPLETE.

                    VOLE
          You will start with science.
          Press Enter to begin.

She walks away, leaving ALEX with the computer. The door slides shut.

                    ALEX
          (Unimpressed) Great...

He reaches out and - unenthusiastically -
presses ENTER.

                              HARD CUT TO:

83   **COMPUTER ANIMATION - OUTER SPACE**   83

From a selection of menus on the screen,
"SPACE" becomes highlighted.

A star field sparkles as a figure floats out.

A voice-over points out aspects of the
view, facts about space, etc.

The figure is ALEX. He is wearing his normal clothes. ALEX looks down to see the
earth below. He is having a wonderful time.

As ALEX floats in space a shadow falls across
him and he looks up. He is in the path of a
SATELLITE, which drifts closer. ALEX is star-
tled as it looms over him. He ducks.

CUT TO ALEX IN THE CHAMBER

ALEX flinches and remembers it's only a program, hits a button.

CUT TO:

84   **COMPUTER ANIMATION - ROMAN VILLA**   84

ALEX finds himself wandering through a Roman landscape. The sound of Roman music (soft, gentle) and GIRLS giggling.

> PROFESSOR'S VOICE-OVER
> The vestal virgins were the most beautiful women in ancient Rome.

> COMPUTER PROGRAM VOICE-OVER
> Turn left for the vestal virgins. Turn left for the vestal virgins.

We hear ALEX'S voice offscreen.

> ALEX
> (voice-over)
> Oh yes...

ALEX turns left. At once, a ROMAN CENTURION leaps out and challenges him.

> PROFESSOR'S VOICE-OVER
> Seeing the vestal virgins was punishable by death.

The ROMAN CENTURION charges at ALEX. ALEX reacts by ducking and weaving as the sword flashes through the air, inches from his head.

CUT TO ALEX IN THE STORMBREAKER

He's ducking and weaving in time with the fight.

CUT TO ALEX IN THE ROMAN SCENE

There's no escape. The CENTURION has him cornered and is coming in for the kill. ALEX reaches up and finds a word. EXIT. He punches the EXIT sign and disappears.

CUT TO:

85   **COMPUTER ANIMATION - DINOSAUR**   85

ALEX appears through dense foliage.

We see from his POV that he has been trans-ported back to a prehistoric age as he can see a BABY TRICERATOPS walk in the dis-tance.

ALEX whistles across the valley.

ALEX waits for a reaction, gives a low growl.

A T-REX suddenly appears right in front of him, snapping its jaws.

CUT TO:

86   **INT.   SAYLE ENTERPRISES - CHAMBER   DAY.**   86

With a jerk, ALEX snatches off the headset. He's glad to find he's safe. For a moment he gazes at the computer screen (blank again). He is impressed, despite himself.

He looks around. He is on his own.

CUT TO:

87   **INT. SAYLE ENTERPRISES - VENTILATION AREA DAY.**   87

Huge VENTILATION FANS turn slowly in the background as ALEX makes his way across a wide, open area.

Two GUARDS approach. ALEX ducks out of sight. He sees a door behind him, chooses his moment, and darts through it.

CUT TO:

88   **INT. SAYLE ENTERPRISES - SUBTERRANEAN COMPLEX DAY.**   88

ALEX finds himself high above a sunken world
of gantries, tangled pipes, girders, and
walkways. Far below him, there's an open
area, and as he watches, DARRIUS SAYLE
appears, to be greeted by a group of SCIEN-
TISTS...men in white coats.

>   SCIENTIST
>   Good morning, Mr. Sayle.

>   SAYLE
>   Is it ready for me?

>   SCIENTIST
>   (Nervous) Yes, sir. This
>   way, please...

SAYLE and the SCIENTISTS walk off. ALEX
wants to know what they're going to
examine. He looks around him. There
are GUARDS everywhere. He can't risk
the stairs or the elevators. What's the
fastest way down?

ANOTHER ANGLE. ALEX grips hold of a vertical
metal girder that runs all the way down.
Gritted teeth. Can he really do this? Yes...

ALEX slides fifty meters down to the bottom. The GUARDS don't see him. He follows
DARRIUS SAYLE.

CUT TO:

89   **INT. SAYLE ENTERPRISES - RESEARCH AREA   DAY.**   89

A corridor leads to another chamber, where DAR-
RIUS SAYLE is examining a sophisticated model.
ALEX will see this again later, but right
now he doesn't recognize it. It's a glass-and-
steel structure. The SCIENTIST presses a button
and the structure opens, allowing a complicated
radio transmitter to rise upward.

                        SCIENTIST
          ...the backup system. It
          will send out a signal that
          will instantly activate all
          seventy thousand computers.
          Of course, it shouldn't be
          needed.

                        SAYLE
          No. It's excellent. This is
          very good.

SAYLE turns around, sensing something. ALEX
hides behind a pillar. He wonders what he's
just been looking at.

                                        CUT TO:

90   **INT.   SAYLE ENTERPRISES - CHAMBER   DAY.**   90

NADIA VOLE has returned to check on ALEX.

                        VOLE
          Kevin...

She is surprised to find the room empty and
at once her suspicions are aroused.

                                        CUT TO:

91   **INT. SAYLE ENTERPRISES - SUBTERRANEAN   91
     COMPLEX   DAY.**

ALEX arrives at a metal door. A sign reads:
RESTRICTED AREA

That's good enough for him. He continues
down a flight of stairs. About halfway down,
the wall changes to rough stone. Wooden
supports shore up the passage...it's obvious
that the corridor has become an old mine
shaft. ALEX continues, cautiously.

ALEX arrives at a door. It is locked. There's
a code box set in the wall. ALEX considers
it...but then he hears footsteps coming from
behind him.

ALEX notices a niche in the rock and ducks
into it just as the two armed GUARDS
appear, coming down the stairs toward the
door.

The two GUARDS stop beside the door. One
of them punches his code into the keypad
and the door slides open.

ALEX looks through the door.

The passageway bends around and he can't
see much. But there's a hint of highly
sophisticated equipment and he can also
hear the hum of machinery. In the distance, an amplified voice echoes out.

> VOICE
> Thirty-nine hours to final
> delivery. Thirty-nine hours
> and counting...

The GUARDS walk on. The doors slide shut.
ALEX darts out of the niche. And suddenly -
a shock - NADIA VOLE is there. Right up close.

> VOLE
> Kevin...? What are you
> doing down here?

> ALEX
> I just wondered where this
> went. What is this place?

> VOLE
> This area is restricted.
> (Beat) Please, this way...

She gestures and ALEX climbs back up the
ramp. NADIA VOLE watches him with even more
suspicion.

                                    CUT TO:

92 **INT.   BROOKLAND SCHOOL - CORRIDOR DAY.**   92

A SCHOOL CLASS is heading into the playground

for a tennis lesson. SABINA follows, momentarily on her own. She is seen by the
TEACHER who taught ALEX. The STORMBREAKER
poster is on the wall.

>   TEACHER
>   Sabina! (A smile) One more
>   day to go.

>   SABINA
>   Until what?

The TEACHER nods at the poster.

>   SABINA
>   I'm not going to be there.
>   I have a riding lesson.

>   TEACHER
>   During school?

>   SABINA
>   I'm hoping to get into the
>   junior championships.

>   TEACHER
>   Oh yes. Well, good night...

As he moves off—

>   SABINA
>   Sir...?

He stops.

>   SABINA
>   You don't know when Alex is
>   coming back?

>   TEACHER
>   Rider? I heard it's mumps.
>   Poor chap. He's going to
>   miss it too.

The TEACHER continues on his way.

CUT TO:

93 **INT.   SAYLE'S HOUSE - ALEX'S ROOM   EVENING.** 93

The door of the room opens and NADIA VOLE comes in. She is obviously up to no good, snooping around, looking for evidence against ALEX.

She sees ALEX'S cell phone. VOLE smiles to herself and picks it up.

CUT TO:

94 **INT.   SAYLE'S HOUSE - MAIN ROOM   EVENING.** 94

Dinner has been served. SAYLE and ALEX are sitting at the oversize table. MR. GRIN pours the wine for SAYLE.

                    SAYLE
          I was brought up on what
          you'd call the wrong side
          of the tracks. In South
          L.A. A real tough neigh-
          borhood. People wouldn't
          even talk to you unless it
          was to make death threats.

                    ALEX
          So what happened?

                    SAYLE
          My mom won a million dol-
          lars on the California
          State Lottery. That's when
          she decided to get me away
          from all that and to have
          me educated in the best
          schooling system in the
          world - here in the UK.

                    ALEX
          You were at school with the
          prime minister.

                    SAYLE
That's right. And he treated
me with the same kindness as
all the other kids in my class.
(Beat) So tell me, how did you
like the Stormbreaker?

                    ALEX
It's cool.

                    SAYLE
Cool. Is that all you can
say? You know, Kevin, it
strikes me that you don't
talk very much like a computer enthusiast. Nor do
you look like one.

                    ALEX
I'd have said the same
about you, Mr. Sayle.

                    SAYLE
You have a point. I've very
much enjoyed meeting you.
I'm sure you'll have a lot
to talk about when you get
back to school.

                    ALEX
Sure.

                    SAYLE
And when we launch the
Stormbreakers - tomorrow -
I'll be thinking particu-
larly of you.

                                    CUT TO:

95 **INT.   SAYLE ENTERPRISES - SUBTERRANEAN   95
        COMPLEX   EVENING**

NADIA VOLE is with one of the SCIENTISTS that
ALEX saw earlier. She watches as ALEX'S cell
phone is hooked up to a computer.

The SCIENTIST rapidly enters some instructions, his fingers rattling over the
keyboard - and a number comes up on a
computer screen.

                    SCIENTIST
        This is the number, Miss Vole.

The SCIENTIST enters more instructions. An
address comes up on the screen.

                    SCIENTIST
        And this phone is regis-
        tered to an address in
        Chelsea.

NADIA VOLE takes one look, then picks up a
telephone.

                    VOLE
        (On the phone) Prepare the
        helicopter.

                                    CUT TO:

96 **EXT.   SAYLE'S HOUSE   NIGHT.**   96

An ARMED GUARD is patrolling the grounds.

                                    CUT TO:

97 **INT.   SAYLE'S HOUSE - ALEX'S ROOM   NIGHT.** 97

ALEX seems to be asleep. But then he throws
back the covers and rolls out of bed, fully
dressed.

ALEX goes over to the door. He tries to
open it. It's locked.

ANOTHER ANGLE. ALEX snatches up the YO-YO
that SMITHERS gave him.

ANOTHER ANGLE. ALEX presses the YO-YO
against a metal fitting. We hear the strong
magnetic casing click into place.

CUT TO:

98 **EXT.   SAYLE'S HOUSE   NIGHT.**   98

A GUARD on patrol passes the side of the house.

ANOTHER ANGLE. ALEX "walks" down the side of
the house. At first sight, it looks impossible.
Then we see a cord connected to his belt,
leading in through the open window of his room.

CUT TO:

99 **INT.   SAYLE'S HOUSE - ALEX'S ROOM   NIGHT.** 99

The YO-YO is still attached to the metal
fitting. It is turning, the miniaturized
engine slowly unspooling a length of the
cord that stretches out through the open
window.

CUT TO:

100 **EXT.   SAYLE'S HOUSE   NIGHT.**   100

ALEX reaches the grass. He straightens up,
unhooks himself, and runs forward. At the
same time, he hears a loud noise: a CARGO
PLANE coming in to land.

CUT TO:

101 **EXT.   SAYLE ENTERPRISES - RUNWAY   NIGHT.** 101

Ten o'clock. A HELICOPTER has landed on the
runway. There are lights everywhere. The
whole place has come to life.

ANOTHER ANGLE. ALEX arrives and hides
behind some crates. Three TRUCKS arrive -
a miniature convoy - and GUARDS driving
FORKLIFT TRUCKS move forward to unload
them. Other GUARDS keep watch.

A man steps into the light. It is YASSEN
GREGOROVICH. He is in total command.

                    YASSEN
          Let's start.

ALEX watches as a series of futuristic
METAL CONTAINERS are forklifted from the
TRUCKS. He sees R5 printed on the side of
each CONTAINER. What the hell is going on?

ANOTHER ANGLE. DARRIUS SAYLE arrives,
being driven in a HUMMER. The strange METAL
CONTAINERS are still being unloaded.

                    SAYLE
          (Jovial) Mr. Gregorovich!

ALEX has heard the name.

                    SAYLE
          I'm glad you were able to
          join us tonight. I didn't
          realize you were going to
          come personally.

                    YASSEN
          This is the last batch. My
          people   wanted   to   be
          assured that the operation
          had all gone according to
          plan.

                    SAYLE
          My plan. My operation. Why
          should your people think that
          anything might go wrong?

And it's at that exact moment that a GUARD,
driving a FORKLIFT TRUCK, drops one of the
containers.

Everyone   freezes.   SAYLE   spins   around,
furious...but also afraid.

YASSEN rushes forward to examine the con-
tainer. SAYLE a few steps behind him.
YASSEN crouches down. Everyone is tense.
But then he straightens up.

                    YASSEN
          It's all right. The con-
          tainer isn't compromised.

A general release of tension. Especially
from the GUARD who dropped the container.

                    GUARD
          I'm sorry. I won't do that
          again.

                    YASSEN
          No. You won't.

YASSEN produces a gun and points it at the man.

ANGLE ON ALEX. As the shot is fired, he flinches.
He can't believe what he's just seen.

ANGLE ON YASSEN. The window of the FORK-
LIFT TRUCK is spider-glassed.

                    YASSEN
          My people don't like mistakes.

SAYLE scowls. The GUARDS continue unloading the
canisters - but with greater care than ever.

REACTION ON ALEX. Everything has changed
now. It's no longer a game - if it ever was.
He knows that he is in the middle of something very dangerous.

                              CUT TO:

102 **INT/EXT.   BLUNT'S CAR/STREET   NIGHT.**   102

ALAN BLUNT is in black tie - and angry. MRS.
JONES is with him as he is driven away at speed.

                    BLUNT
          I told you I didn't want to
          be interrupted...

                    MRS. JONES
          ...unless it was important.

                    BLUNT
And is it?

                    MRS. JONES
We just got this from Alex
Rider.

She hands him a written report.

                    BLUNT
Yassen Gregorovich...

                    MRS. JONES
It has to be.

                    BLUNT
I thought he was still in
North Korea.

                    MRS. JONES
It seems not. (beat) This
is the proof you need.
The Stormbreaker launch is
less than 24 hours away.
Cancel it.

                    BLUNT
Yes. You're right. I'll put
a call into Downing Street.

                    MRS. JONES
And get Alex out.

                    BLUNT
There's no need to.
He'll be flying out at
twelve o'clock tomorrow.
You can meet him if you
like. Take him out for
an ice cream.

A look from MRS. JONES.

                    BLUNT
He's done very well. He
deserves a treat.

CUT TO:

103 **INT.   IAN RIDER'S HOUSE   NIGHT.**   103

JACK STARBRIGHT is varnishing the FUGU FISH
from her sushi dinner, turning it into an
ornament. At the same time, she's watching
a SUMO WRESTLING FIGHT on television. The
doorbell rings.

JACK picks up the REMOTE CONTROL and
turns the volume down on the TV. Then
she crosses the hall and opens the door
to find a smartly dressed NADIA VOLE on
the doorstep. The time is about 10:30 p.m.

                    VOLE
          Excuse me. I'm looking for
          a person called Jack.

                    JACK
          Is this about Alex?

VOLE takes in the name, her suspicions
already aroused.

                    VOLE
          (Sly) Yes, it is.

                    JACK
          Then you'd better come in.

CUT TO:

104 **INT.   IAN RIDER'S HOUSE - LIVING ROOM   NIGHT.** 104

NADIA VOLE comes into the room with JACK.

                    VOLE
          You are a friend of Alex?

                    JACK
          I look after him.

NADIA notices another photograph of ALEX and
IAN RIDER on the side table. She picks it up.

                    VOLE
         This is Alex!

                    JACK
         Yes.

                    VOLE
         And this man with him.
         (Realizes) His father.

                    JACK
         (Taking the photograph) His
         uncle! Look...what's this
         about?

NADIA VOLE produces a gun and points it at JACK.

                    VOLE
         Alex Rider. Tell me...who is
         this boy? What is he doing?

                    JACK
         Who are you?

                    VOLE
         Who is he working for?

                    JACK
         I'm not going to tell you
         anything!

JACK lashes out with the photograph and
catches NADIA VOLE by surprise. VOLE fires,
but the bullet goes wild. The gun flies out
of her hand, sliding across the floor.

JACK backs away from NADIA VOLE, who
advances on her menacingly.

                    JACK
         I should warn you, I have a
         black belt in karate. At
         least, I went out with a
         guy who had a black belt in
         karate - and he taught me
         how to look after myself...

NADIA VOLE throws herself at JACK. Her foot comes down on the REMOTE CONTROL and the TV short-circuits. The image changes - and throughout the fight changes and changes again. These are examples...

ON THE TV: Homer Simpson going "Doh!"

NADIA reaches out and grabs the sushi knife that JACK was using in the first scene. NADIA comes at her with the sushi knife, slashing the air inches from her.

ON THE TV: Almost the identical movements in a late-night movie.

The fight continues. But we keep CUTTING BACK to the TV which offers its own ironic commentary on the action with dozens of images...

JOHN CLEESE hitting MICHAEL PALIN with a large fish (Monty Python).

A POKER PLAYER: "Hit me!"

OZZY OSBOURNE - punch-drunk, dazed.

A famous POLITICIAN striking the table with his fist to make a point.

THE SUMO WRESTLERS (again).

NADIA swings the knife and decapitates a potted plant. She slices an entire curtain in two. She chops a standard lamp in half. But keeps missing JACK.

JACK has no weapon. But then she sees the FUGU FISH which she was varnishing. She picks it up by the nose and throws it...

The FUGU FISH flies across the room. Its vicious spikes bury themselves in NADIA'S hand. NADIA cries out and drops the knife.

JACK makes a dive for the gun and scoops it up.

> JACK
> All right. That's enough.

But NADIA VOLE is already on her way out. In pain. The door swings shut behind her. JACK is relieved to see her go.

CUT TO:

105 **INT.   SAYLE'S HOUSE - MAIN ROOM   DAY.**   105

The following morning. We're on DARRIUS SAYLE, who is sitting in a comfortable chair, being given a manicure by a PRETTY GIRL. But it's a new DARRIUS SAYLE. The mask has slipped. The monster is loose.

> SAYLE
> Alex Rider.

NADIA VOLE is reporting to her employer.

> VOLE
> I suspected him from the moment he arrived.

> SAYLE
> And his uncle was Ian Rider, the security guard who was actually a spy!

CUT TO:

106 **INT.   SAYLE'S HOUSE - ALEX'S ROOM   DAY.**   106

ALEX is in his room, listening in with his NIN-TENDO DS device - connected by headphones. The screen shows a GRAPHIC IMAGE of the room, and the position of SAYLE and NADIA VOLE inside.

> SAYLE
> (voice only)
> These people! I mean, really...!

>   VOLE
> What do you want me to do?

                              CUT TO:

107 **INT.   SAYLE'S HOUSE - MAIN ROOM   DAY.**   107

SAYLE and VOLE continue their discussion.

>   SAYLE
> Go to his room. Wake him up
> gently. Try not to alarm
> him. (beat) Then kill him.

>   VOLE
> Whatever you say, Mr. Sayle.

>   SAYLE
> And then you'd better get
> that hand seen to, Nadia.
> Right? I need you on top
> form today.

NADIA VOLE raises her hand and we see
that the FUGU FISH has been removed. But
it has left a number of holes in her
hand.

SAYLE examines his own manicured nails.

>   SAYLE
>   Nice.

                              CUT TO:

108 **EXT.   SAYLE ENTERPRISES - CHECKPOINT   DAY.**   108

A small truck passes through the checkpoint
and leaves the compound.

                              CUT TO:

109 **EXT.   CORNISH COUNTRYSIDE   DAY.**   109

The truck follows the road down toward Port
Tallon. But the way ahead is blocked by a FLOCK
OF SHEEP, crossing from one side to another.
The DRIVER slows down, then continues.

ANOTHER ANGLE. ALEX RIDER is revealed. He has climbed out of the back. He stays by the road while the truck drives out of sight. He's carrying his shoulder bag.

CUT TO:

110   **EXT.   THE KERNEWECK SHAFT   DAY.**   110

ALEX walks down a Cornish hill. It's a beautiful day. The countryside at its most Cornish and most gorgeous. The calm before the storm.

ALEX stops and takes out the postcard that IAN RIDER sent him. He examines the picture of the Kerneweck Shaft...

...then lowers it...

...and the actual KERNEWECK SHAFT is right behind it, in the far distance.

CLOSER SHOT. ALEX arrives at the old shaft - a broken brick wall, crumbling tower, and metal lid. ALEX examines the lid. It is locked with a serious padlock.

But ALEX has brought various bits of equipment in his shoulder bag. He kneels beside the metal lid. He has the ZIT CREAM that SMITHERS gave him and squeezes some onto the lock.

A pause. Then a hiss. The padlock dissolves. ALEX slips the ZIT CREAM into his trouser pocket and opens the metal lid.

He looks down. A metal ladder descends into thick, damp darkness. ALEX grits his teeth. He climbs down.

CUT TO:

111   **INT.   THE DOZMARY MINE - FIRST TUNNEL   DAY.** 111

A great metal cylinder, plunging down into the core of the earth. ALEX climbs down, his footsteps echoing. Deeper and deeper. Light pouring in from above.

At last he reaches the bottom of the ladder. Too far down. Here, all is dark. He takes out a flashlight and turns it on, and for a moment he looks like the kid on the covers of all the Alex Rider books.

This is a scary place. Claustrophobic, dark, empty, broken-down. ALEX can hear the drip of water. Old mining works surround him.

He makes sure of his sense of direction. Sets off.

CUT TO:

112 **INT.   THE DOZMARY MINE - SECOND TUNNEL   DAY.** 112

Following the flashlight, ALEX explores the endless darkness of this forgotten, subterranean world. More mine workings. A disused railway. A moldering train and wagon. He turns on the flashlight and...

A SCREAM. Something shoots out of the dark- ness. Blazing eyes and fangs. But it's just a BAT. It flutters away down the tunnel. ALEX lets out a breath.

CUT TO:

113 **INT.   THE DOZMARY MINE - THIRD TUNNEL   DAY.** 113

It's getting deeper, nastier - and more and more narrow! He comes to an area where part of the ceiling has collapsed.

ALEX stops, realizing that the way ahead is nothing more than a black hole, barely big enough to contain him. To continue, he's going to have to bury himself alive.

                    ALEX
          (Muttered) You've got to be
          kidding...

ALEX pushes the backpack ahead of him and squeezes, headfirst, into the hole.

                                        CUT TO:

114 **INT.   THE DOZMARY MINE - SMALL TUNNEL   DAY.**   114

Using his flashlight to show the way, ALEX crawls through this tiny, claustrophobic space. We get a sense of the tons of earth bearing down on him. This is the world's worst "buried alive" nightmare.

It gets worse. As he squirms forward, his movements release a cascade of earth and dust. He chokes. Is the whole ceiling going to cave in on him?

The cascade stops. Desperately, ALEX continues forward.

                                        CUT TO:

115 **INT.   THE DOZMARY MINE - FINAL CHAMBER   DAY.**   115

ALEX punches his way back into the air. It's like a zombie rising from the grave. He stops, spits out dirt, and gasps for breath.

He's in the middle of a large, well-lit chamber. ALEX can hear the hum of machinery. Set in the wall is an industrial fan - blowing warm air into the mine.

ALEX breathes in the air, gratefully.

Then he continues forward and comes to a grille set in the wall. He kneels down beside it and looks through...

                                        CUT TO:

116 **INT.   STORMBREAKER ASSEMBLY LINE   DAY.**   116

A huge reveal. ALEX is looking at the secret assembly line at Sayle Enterprises.

An extraordinary, sweeping underground chamber carved out of the earth with rock walls and industrial lighting. The real work of SAYLE ENTERPRISES takes place here.

The STORMBREAKER COMPUTERS roll along assembly lines. Hundreds of them. We see glistening GLASS PHIALS - the same ones that YASSEN GREGOROVICH brought in by plane. They are marked R5 and contain some sort of liquid. A single, evil-looking machine injects the liquid into the COMPUTERS.

WORKERS oversee the process. ARMED GUARDS watch over the WORKERS, patrolling along iron gantries.

In the distance, two WORKERS dressed in decontamination suits with yellow armbands enter a glass shower and disappear in a burst of chemical steam. There's a glass-fronted control box with MEN IN WHITE COATS keeping a watchful eye on progress.

And in charge of the whole operation: YASSEN GREGOROVICH. Dressed in decontamination clothes. Talking to a MAN IN A WHITE COAT. Giving instructions.

An amplified voice booms out.

                    VOICE
          Final order ready for dis-
          patch. Two hours and twelve
          minutes to departure.

                                        CUT TO:

117 **INT.   THE DOZMARY MINE - FINAL CHAMBER   DAY.** 117

REACTION ON ALEX. He's way out of his depth. And he knows it.

                                        CUT TO:

118 **INT.   STORMBREAKER ASSEMBLY LINE   DAY.** 118

A VENTILATION GRILLE set high up behind a row of lockers. A set of fingers poke through, removing the grille. ALEX looks around, then climbs quickly down.

> VOICE
> Red team report to decontam-
> ination. Red team for
> decontamination.

Two WORKERS in biochemical suits with red armbands walk past ALEX, heading for the steam shower.

ALEX ducks out of the locker area and crouches behind a bank of machinery, tak-ing a closer look.

THE STORMBREAKERS. After the LIQUID has been injected, the WORKERS slide a panel, sealing it in. Finally, the panel is welded shut, brilliant sparks flying off the casing.

ALEX is puzzled. He has to get closer. He moves out of his hiding place...

...backing into a gun that is being pointed at his head. He turns slowly. And finds himself face-to-face with a narrow-eyed GUARD.

A FEW MOMENTS LATER...

ALEX, with two GUARDS now escorting him, stands in front of YASSEN GREGOROVICH. The computers keep sliding past. The glass phials are still being dropped into them.

Incredulous, YASSEN swears to himself in Russian. Then...

> YASSEN
> (To ALEX) What are you
> doing here?

No reply from ALEX. He's looking scared...a lost fourteen-year-old.

                    YASSEN
          Who are you?

                    ALEX
          (Scared) What's going on?
          My name's Kevin Blake. I
          was invited here.

                    YASSEN
          It's a good act. You do it
          very well. But you shouldn't
          have come here...

                    ALEX
          We can talk about this.

                    YASSEN
          I don't think so.

ALEX sees one of the GLASS PHIALS marked
R5. Suddenly he acts. As fast as a snake,
his hand darts out and snatches it.

                    ALEX
          Yes we can.

Everyone freezes, terrified. ALEX has the
upper hand.

                    YASSEN
          Don't drop that!

                    ALEX
          R5. What is it?

                    YASSEN
          Put it back...

                    ALEX
          What's the way out of here?

YASSEN gestures toward a door up a flight
of stairs, along a gantry.

                    YASSEN
          (Pointing) There.

                         ALEX
          Thanks.

ALEX tosses the GLASS PHIAL at YASSEN and
runs. YASSEN'S eyes widen as he reaches out
and catches the PHIAL. If this man has ever
been scared in his life, that moment has
just happened.

ALEX is halfway up the stairs. But now a
GUARD takes out his automatic machine gun
and opens fire. Bullets fly, ricocheting
off the metal stairs all around ALEX.

YASSEN steps forward quickly and stops the
GUARD from firing.

                    YASSEN
          Stop. What are you doing,
          you idiot! You can't fire
          bullets in here!

                    GUARD
          Of course. I'm sorry. I
          won't do that again.

The GUARD realizes what he's just said
(exactly the same words as the guard on the
runway). Slowly, he meets YASSEN'S eyes.

                                   CUT TO:

119 **INT. SAYLE ENTERPRISES - DOOR   DAY**   119

ALEX reaches the door that barred his way
when he was on the other side. But he can
open it from this side. He hurries through.

                                   CUT TO:

120 **INT.   SAYLE ENTERPRISES - SUBTERRANEAN**   120
     COMPLEX   DAY.

ALEX RIDER finds himself at the bottom of
the massive, subterranean complex where he
saw SAYLE with the scientists. The only way

is up! More GUARDS appear, searching for him.

ALEX reaches into his backpack and takes out the NINTENDO DS. He inserts the GREEN SCREEN cartridge and slides the whole thing across the floor.

The GUARDS see the device. Before they can do anything, there's an explosion. Suddenly they are surrounded by choking GREEN SMOKE. ALEX climbs up as the GUARDS fire blind.

CUT TO:

121   **EXT. SAYLE ENTERPRISES - VENTILATION AREA   DAY.**   121

For a moment it looks as if ALEX has gotten away. There's nobody in sight. Cautiously, he moves forward.

And then we see that NADIA VOLE is standing on a gallery above him.

> VOLE
> Going somewhere?

NADIA has taken off the bandage. Her hand not only has ugly, red holes but is quite swollen from the poison in the FUGU FISH.

> ALEX
> Yeah. I have a plane to catch.

> VOLE
> Not anymore.

Suddenly there are GUARDS everywhere. ALEX sees that he is totally surrounded.

CUT TO:

122   **INT.   SAYLE ENTERPRISES - MAIN ROOM   DAY.**   122

ALEX is tied to a heavy, wooden chair. DARRIUS SAYLE - immaculately turned out for his coming presentation with the PRIME MINISTER -

and MR. GRIN confront him. NADIA VOLE
to one side. The JELLYFISH floats silently in
the background. Two ARMED GUARDS on the door.

> SAYLE
> What is your name?

> ALEX
> You know who I am. I won
> the competition...

> SAYLE
> Mr. Grin...

MR. GRIN takes out a knife. A flash of silver and the blade buries itself in the back
of ALEX'S seat, inches from his head.

> ALEX
> If this is how you treat the
> winner, I'd hate to see what
> happened to the runner-up.

> VOLE
> You're not Kevin Blake.
> You're Alex Rider.

> ALEX
> If you already know, why
> are you asking?

> VOLE
> Your uncle was pretending
> to be a security man. Yassen
> Gregorovich dealt with him.

ALEX can't disguise the hurt he feels,
hearing this. SAYLE sees the reaction.

> SAYLE
> And MI6 sent you to take
> his place? (beat) Sending
> a fourteen-year-old to do
> their dirty work. Not very
> British, I'd have said, you
> know? Not cricket!

                    ALEX
          What are you doing here?
          You're putting a virus into
          the Stormbreaker.

ALEX suddenly realizes.

                    ALEX
          (Horrified as he gradually
          realizes the truth.) But it's
          not a computer virus. It's
          the real thing!

                    SAYLE
          It's called R5. It's been
          genetically modified. It's
          nasty. It's very nasty.

                    ALEX
          Why are you doing this?

                    SAYLE
          I'll tell you! I'll be delighted!

A beat. SAYLE relishes the moment.

                    SAYLE
          Do you know what it's like
          to be a foreigner in this
          country? An American in
          Paris...that's a musical. But
          an American in London...for
          me that was slow death. I was
          mocked and derided from the
          day I arrived. Even at
          school. Especially at school.
          The other kids stole my
          books. They put pins on my
          chair. They called me trailer
          boy. Darrius Smell...you
          know why?

                    ALEX
          Because you didn't wash?

SAYLE raises a hand and for a moment we really believe he is going to slap ALEX - hard -

across the face. But at the last second, he
manages to regain control. He lowers the hand.

                    SAYLE
          Because they were snobs.
          (beat) There were many chil-
          dren I hated at that school
          but there was one who was
          worse than any of them. And
          do you know who he was? Do
          you know who he grew up to
          be? (beat) The prime minis-
          ter. That's who! All my life
          I've been treated the same
          way. No matter how rich I am
          or how successful I've
          become. I'm still Darrius
          Smell, the trailer boy.

                    ALEX
          (Astounded) And that's
          what this is all about?
          Revenge?

                    SAYLE
          In just a few hours' time,
          at the Science Museum in
          London, my old friend the
          prime minister will press
          the button that will con-
          nect all the Stormbreakers
          on my wireless network. And
          at the same moment, he will
          release the virus straight
          into classes packed with
          British schoolchildren!

                    ALEX
          You're going to kill thou-
          sands of people!

                    SAYLE
          No! No! Of course not! I'm
          going to kill millions of them!

ALEX stares in horror.

                    ALEX
          You're not serious!

                    SAYLE
          You don't think so?

                    ALEX
          You were bullied at school.
          Lots of people are bullied at
          school. But it doesn't turn
          them into raving psychopaths.

Another glint of silver as a knife flashes
through the air. It buries itself in the
seat between ALEX'S legs, half an inch from
his crotch.

                    SAYLE
          You should be careful how
          you talk to me.

                    ALEX
          That was a good shot.

                    MR. GRIN
          Eurgh.

                    SAYLE
          Actually, it was a near miss.
          It's time to say good-bye,
          Alex. As you may have seen,
          I'm packing up and leaving.
          I'd love to stay and watch,
          but I have a rather important
          appointment in London, so I'll
          leave you to Nadia.

NADIA VOLE steps forward - a demon from
hell. Now we see her injured hand. It has
gotten considerably worse.

                                   CUT TO:

123 **INT.   MI6 - OPERATIONS AREA   DAY.**   123

     BLUNT and MRS. JONES emerge from an eleva-
     tor and walk together. A sense of urgency.

> BLUNT
> They won't listen to us.

> MRS. JONES
> What?

> BLUNT
> You know the government
> view of intelligence at the
> moment. They'd sooner trust
> a Ouija board. The bottom
> line is that they're ignor-
> ing my advice and going
> ahead with the ceremony.

> MRS. JONES
> Security?

> BLUNT
> I'm throwing a net around
> the Science Museum, but it
> may be beside the point.

> MRS. JONES
> What about Alex? He wasn't
> on the twelve o'clock plane.

> BLUNT
> Let's hope he can look
> after himself.

CUT TO:

124 **INT.   SAYLE'S HOUSE - AQUARIUM   DAY.**   124

SPLASH!

Alex plunges into the water and twists
down, surrounded by swirling bubbles. He
looks up and sees the JELLYFISH above him.
His eyes widen in shock. He kicks back.
There's enough room in the giant tank to
avoid the creature. Just.

CUT TO:

125 **INT.   SAYLE'S HOUSE - MAIN ROOM   DAY.**   125

NADIA VOLE stands on the other side of the glass, watching.

>   NADIA
> The jellyfish cannot attack
> you, Alex. It has, as you
> said, no brains. But you
> will tire soon. You will
> drift into its embrace. And
> then...

NADIA VOLE smiles. She produces a camera. She takes a (flash) snapshot of ALEX. This is difficult and painful for her as her hand is now quite seriously deformed.

>   NADIA
> A souvenir. For Mr. Sayle.

                                    CUT TO:

126 **EXT.   SAYLE ENTERPRISES   DAY.**   126

The evacuation continues. MR. GRIN, now wearing an old-fashioned pilot's headgear and jacket, climbs into the CARGO PLANE.

                                    CUT TO:

127 **INT.   SAYLE'S HOUSE - AQUARIUM   DAY.**   127

ALEX looks around him. Glass all around. Nothing over his head, no way of climbing out. NADIA VOLE still watching. Almost as horrible as the JELLYFISH. And the JELLY-FISH is horribly close. The tentacles hang down.

A tentacle drifts in the current and almost touches his arm. ALEX winces and pulls away. NADIA VOLE takes a photograph.

ALEX notices the frame of the aquarium. It's solid metal with rivets. At last he knows what to do. Still watching the JELLYFISH, he takes out the ZIT CREAM.

NADIA VOLE is puzzled, suspicious.

ALEX takes a breath and dives down. Underwater, underneath the JELLYFISH, he smears
the cream onto the metal frame. Nothing
happens. But then we see bubbles rising as
the metal begins to burn.

                              CUT TO:

128 **INT.   SAYLE'S HOUSE - MAIN ROOM   DAY.**   128

NADIA VOLE is alarmed.

                    VOLE
          What are you doing, *du ver-*
          dammtes kind...?

And then, an explosion. The entire tank
simply bursts, thousands of gallons of
water engulfing the room (and VOLE). The
JELLYFISH going with it.

ALEX'S POINT OF VIEW. A vortex. He's blinded. Thrown helplessly forward.

ALEX recovers. He's on the carpet now.
Soaked. There's water everywhere. But no
sign of the JELLYFISH. He turns
around...

...and sees NADIA VOLE, still sitting in
the chair, now in a terrible embrace with
the JELLYFISH. She is smothered by it, her
stockinged legs poking out from the mass
of tentacles and jelly, twitching.

ALEX reacts. With disgust. He snatches
one of the HARPOON GUNS off the wall and
hurries out.

                              CUT TO:

129 **EXT.   SAYLE ENTERPRISES   DAY.**   129

Lots of activity outside as people leave.
JEEPS, TRUCKS, GUARDS on foot, all evacuate
Sayle Enterprises. The CARGO PLANE is taxi-
ing onto the runway.

ALEX appears, carrying the HARPOON GUN and
wearing the SMITHERS backpack. He sees the
CARGO PLANE at the end of the runway.

And then an alarm goes off - and at that
moment he's seen. A GUARD opens fire. ALEX
throws himself behind a series of oil drums
as the bullets explode around him.

CLOSE ON MR. GRIN at the controls of the
CARGO PLANE. A final test of the ailerons...

A GUARD talks into a radio transmitter. The
first GUARD fires again. Bullets strafe the
oil drums.

ALEX emerges from behind the oilcans on one
of the QUAD BIKES we saw earlier.

More GUARDS open fire. ALEX races toward
the runway. Bullets tear up the concrete.

MR. GRIN pushes down on the thrust levers
and the CARGO PLANE begins to take off.
It's hurtling down the runway toward
ALEX.

GUARDS IN JEEPS descending on ALEX from
three sides. ALEX has made it to the runway. The CARGO PLANE is in front of him

MR. GRIN at the controls. Pulling on the
joystick, the plane rises over ALEX.

The THREE JEEPS are getting closer. ALEX
stops, takes out the HARPOON, aims at the
CARGO PLANE, and fires.

The HARPOON hits the CARGO PLANE.

ALEX is yanked off the QUAD BIKE. He's like
a doll, dangling in the air at the end of
the harpoon.

The three JEEPS try to stop. Too late. They
crash into one another spectacularly. An
explosion and a ball of flame.

The CARGO PLANE has gone. ALEX has gone with it, rising above the flames.

ANOTHER ANGLE. YASSEN GREGOROVICH drives up in a HUMMER and stops. He sees the chaos. The smashed-up jeeps. The disappearing plane with ALEX dangling underneath it.

His eyes show a wary respect.

                                    CUT TO:

130   **INT.   CARGO PLANE   DAY.**   130

ALEX has managed to open a door and crawls into the plane. He sees that many of the contents of the house fill the belly of the aircraft - including artworks, furniture, the snooker table.

MR. GRIN is strapped into the pilot's seat. He is unaware that ALEX is on board.

ALEX takes out the FOUNTAIN PEN that SMITHERS gave him. He points it at MR. GRIN and presses a button on the side.

The NIB shoots out of the PEN and hits MR. GRIN in the neck. MR. GRIN cries out...

...but before he can do more, his eyeballs dilate and change color. The drug is taking effect.

ANOTHER ANGLE. On ALEX. He's not certain the pen device has actually worked.

                    ALEX
          All right, Mr. Grin. I want
          you to fly me to London. As
          fast as you can.

                    MR. GRIN
          Yargh...

MR. GRIN turns the joystick and the plane changes direction, heading for London.

ALEX is still holding the pen - now without a nib. He breathes a sigh of relief.

                              CUT TO:

131 **EXT.   HYDE PARK, LONDON   DAY.**   131

A motor cavalcade. The PRIME MINISTER is on
his way to the Science Museum. POLICE CYCLISTS
escort him. He passes a group of HORSE RIDERS
having a lesson in Hyde Park.

Curiously, the CAMERA slides over to them. And
we discover SABINA PLEASURE having a lesson
with four other GIRLS and a posh INSTRUCTOR.

                    INSTRUCTOR
          Keep that back straight,
          Sabina. Now, we're all going
          to have a little trot...

                              CUT TO:

132 **EXT.   THE SCIENCE MUSEUM   DAY.**   132

There's a crowd outside the science museum
and a sense of excitement. PHOTOGRAPHERS.
flash their cameras as a black limousine
pulls up and the PRIME MINISTER gets out.
He is surrounded by SPIN DOCTORS and CIVIL
SERVANTS.

The PRIME MINISTER smiles for the cameras
and goes into the museum.

                              CUT TO:

133 **INT.   THE SCIENCE MUSEUM - EAST HALL   DAY.** 133

A huge chamber with a platform set up in
the center and a ceremonial button to
press. The button is connected to a lumi-
nous RADIO TRANSMITTING DEVICE.

Lots of security. Armed POLICE and SPECIAL
FORCES MEN look down from vantage points. JOUR-
NALISTS and VIPS are taking their seats, which

have been arranged in front of the platform.

MRS. JONES and ALAN BLUNT make their way to their seats. They're wary, waiting for trouble. They find their way blocked by JACK STARBRIGHT.

>   JACK
>   Where's Alex?

>   MRS. JONES
>   We don't know.

>   JACK
>   What do you mean, you don't
>   know? You   promised   me
>   you'd look after him...!

Then...applause from the CROWD.

>   BLUNT
>   We don't have time for this
>   now, Miss Starbright.

>   MRS. JONES
>   The prime minister...

The PRIME MINISTER has come in from the street. At the same time, DARRIUS SAYLE walks onto the platform. The two men shake hands. More cameras flash.

>   CUT TO:

134 **EXT.   AIRSPACE OVER LONDON   DAY.**   134

The CARGO PLANE approaches the center of London. Various landmarks (St. Paul's, the Millennium Wheel) can be seen in the distance.

>   CUT TO:

135 **INT.   CARGO PLANE   DAY.**   135

ALEX presses a button and electronically opens a huge door at the back of the cargo plane. A panoramic view of London is revealed. Wind and clouds rush past. A drugged MR. GRIN is still flying the plane.

> ALEX
> (To MR. GRIN) OK. I want you to keep flying north until you run out of fuel. Then you can land.

> MR. GRIN
> Norgh...

ALEX goes to the edge of the plane. He has to grit himself for this. He's a very long way up. He's never parachuted before. A last sigh of regret. Why me? He jumps...

> CUT TO:

136 **EXT.   AIRSPACE OVER LONDON   DAY.**   136

ALEX falls through the sky over London. He uses his arms to steer himself. The CARGO PLANE disappears into the distance, heading north.

> CUT TO:

137 **INT.   THE SCIENCE MUSEUM - EAST HALL   DAY.** 137

The PRIME MINISTER is giving a speech, standing underneath the STORMBREAKER letters. JACK STARBRIGHT, ALAN BLUNT, and MRS. JONES in the audience.

> PRIME MINISTER
> The message is quite clear. Education. Education. And...

He loses his place. Turns the page of his speech and picks it up again.

> PRIME MINISTER
> ...and education.

The PRESS SECRETARY rolls his eyes. He knows the man is an idiot.

                    PRIME MINISTER
         And that is why I am
         delighted to accept the
         generous offer made by one
         of our foremost entrepre-
         neurs and my old school
         colleague, Darrius Smell.

A terrible error. The PRIME MINISTER quickly
recovers.

                    PRIME MINISTER
         Sayle! Darrius Sayle!

Applause as SAYLE takes the stage. He stands
next to the PRIME MINISTER.

                              CUT TO:

138 **EXT.   AIRSPACE OVER LONDON   DAY.**   138

All of LONDON is spread out below. But
ALEX has got the SCIENCE MUSEUM in his
sights. He pulls a cord on his backpack
and a PARACHUTE billows out. We hear
the CLICKING and WHIRRING of CAMERAS.

                              CUT TO:

139 **INT.   THE SCIENCE MUSEUM - EAST HALL   DAY.** 139

The PHOTOGRAPHERS in the museum are taking
dozens of snaps. SAYLE is now making his
speech, standing next to the prime minister.

                    SAYLE
         It is the prime minister who
         must take credit for what's
         about to happen here.

                              CUT TO:

140 **INT.   SCHOOLROOM   DAY.**   140

A class of CHILDREN are watching the
broadcast live on television. There's a

teacher with them. A shining STORMBREAKER
is on the table in front of them.

> SAYLE
> (On-screen) As I promised,
> my Stormbreakers are about
> to transform the lives of
> every child in Britain.

CUT TO:

141 **INT.   SCHOOL ASSEMBLY   DAY.**   141

Another school and an assembly room filled
with SCHOOLCHILDREN watching the broadcast
on TV. A TEACHER stands next to their brand-
new STORMBREAKER.

> SAYLE
> (voice only)
> This is a day that none of
> you will ever forget.

CUT TO:

142 **INT.   BROOKLAND SCHOOL - CLASS   DAY.**   142

ALEX'S class is also watching the broadcast
with the TEACHER, GARY (the bully), and the
KIDS we saw in the opening shot.

> SAYLE
> (On-screen) And now I shall ask
> my old friend the prime minis-
> ter to press the button that
> will activate this radio trans-
> mitter. The transmitter will
> send out the signal that will
> activate the Stormbreakers
> across the entire country.

CUT TO:

143 **EXT.   THE SCIENCE MUSEUM - ROOF   DAY.**   143

ALEX is falling faster. He can see the roof
of the SCIENCE MUSEUM rushing up toward him.

CUT TO:

144 **INT.   SCIENCE MUSEUM - EAST HALL   DAY.** 144

DARRIUS SAYLE steps aside.

SAYLE
Prime Minister...

The PRIME MINISTER steps forward. The button is right in front of him.

ANGLE on BLUNT and MRS. JONES. Somehow they know this is a mistake.

Angle on JACK STARBRIGHT, also worried. Back on the PRIME MINISTER.

PRIME MINISTER
Well, here we go, then...

His finger is ready.

CUT TO:

145 **EXT.   THE SCIENCE MUSEUM - ROOF   DAY.**   145

ALEX hits the roof and smashes right through.

CUT TO:

146 **INT.   SCIENCE MUSEUM - EAST HALL   DAY.** 146

ALEX continues his journey down, crashing through the roof of the East Hall. Glass fragments shower down. The AUDIENCE panics - screams of alarm. The PRIME MINISTER freezes. SAYLE looks up in shock.

ALEX'S parachute canopy has gotten caught up with the roof. He dangles in the air like a puppet - but then the canopy begins to rip and gradually he is lowered toward the floor. At the same time, he desperately reaches for the straps, trying to release himself.

ANGLE ON MRS. JONES, the first to react. She speaks into a radio.

> MRS. JONES
> Security alert. Bring him down, now!

JACK STARBRIGHT has overheard this. Is it ALEX? She can't be sure.

> JACK
> No! Wait...!

SPECIAL FORCES TROOPS run toward ALEX. The first of them brings up his machine gun and aims.

At the very last moment, ALEX manages to unfasten himself from his parachute and drops down, catlike, onto the floor. Now he sees the SPECIAL FORCES SOLDIER who's aiming at him.

> ALEX
> Wolf!

Sure enough, it's WOLF. The soldier who trained with him.

ANOTHER ANGLE. JACK STARBRIGHT recognizes ALEX.

> JACK
> (Amazed) Alex?

BACK ON ALEX. WOLF has momentarily frozen. ALEX takes everything in.

> ALEX
> (To WOLF) Your gun!

WOLF hesitates for perhaps half a second. Then he throws his machine gun to ALEX.

ANGLE ON SAYLE. Standing by the PRIME MINISTER.

> SAYLE
> Go on! Press it!

The PRIME MINISTER is rooted to the spot. SAYLE realizes he's going to have to press the button himself.

ANGLE ON ALEX. He aims carefully at the RADIO TRANSMITTING DEVICE and fires... well above the AUDIENCE'S head. It explodes.

The AUDIENCE screams and dives for cover.

The PRIME MINISTER finds himself facing DARRIUS SAYLE.

> PRIME MINISTER
> Darrius...?

> SAYLE
> You...twerp!

DARRIUS SAYLE punches the PRIME MINISTER right on the nose. The PRIME MINISTER falls back. His BODYGUARDS rush to surround him, and in the confusion, SAYLE lunges off the stage.

> CUT TO:

147 **INT.   BROOKLAND SCHOOL - CLASS   DAY.**   147

The BROOKLAND SCHOOLCHILDREN are watching the scene on TV with amazement. The TEACHER and GARY are still there. Then GARY sees ALEX on the bridge. A long shot. Hard to see his face. But...

> GARY
> That's Alex!

Everyone stares.

> TEACHER
> Don't be ridiculous, Gary.
> Alex is in bed with mumps.

GARY scowls.

CUT TO:

148 **INT.   THE SCIENCE MUSEUM - EAST HALL   DAY.**   148

Back at the Science Museum, MRS. JONES and
ALAN BLUNT approach ALEX. JACK STARBRIGHT
is now with him.

> MRS. JONES
> You've done very well,
> Alex. But you should go.

> ALEX
> What about Sayle?

> BLUNT
> You can leave him to us.

> ALEX
> Right.

ALEX hands the machine gun to ALAN BLUNT -
who is very unsure what to do with it. ALEX
leaves with JACK.

CUT TO:

149 **INT/EXT.   JACK'S CAR/LONDON   DAY.**   149

JACK is driving ALEX home. ALEX is angry,
still thinking...

> ALEX
> How could they let him slip
> away?

> JACK
> It's not your problem. I
> can't believe I ever let you
> get mixed up in all this.
> But it's over. It's time you
> came home!

> ALEX
> (Half to himself) Yeah. But
> where's he going?

                    JACK
          Somewhere remote and far
          away where nobody will
          ever find him. Paraguay.
          (beat) Iowa.

A pause.

                    JACK
          By the way, I don't suppose
          you got the phone number of
          that hunky soldier. (beat)
          Do those people have phone
          numbers?

                    ALEX
          Jack! Stop the car!

JACK brakes hard. ALEX is looking out of the
window. There's a clear view across London.

And there it is. Unmistakable.

The distinctive rooftop of SAYLE TOWER.
The same shape as the model that ALEX saw
when he was in Cornwall.

                    ALEX
          That's it!

                    JACK
          What?

                    ALEX
          That building. Sayle Tower.
          He had a model of it in
          Cornwall. He was talking
          about a backup. Something
          about a manual override.
          That's where it is.

JACK looks at him. Suddenly she knows it
isn't over yet.

                    ALEX
          And that's where he is.

He's going to set off the
virus himself.

CUT TO:

150 **EXT.   HYDE PARK, LONDON   DAY.**   150

JACK STARBRIGHT and ALEX speed around a
corner...

...and come to a grinding halt in a major
traffic jam. There seems to be no way out.

>   ALEX
> We're not going to make it.

ALEX looks around him. A group of HORSE
RIDERS - a posh riding school - crosses in
front of the car. Then he sees...

...but that's impossible! SABINA PLEASURE
is among them, on her horse. ALEX opens the
car door.

>   JACK
> Alex...?

>   ALEX
> That's Sabina!

ALEX rushes over to SABINA.

>   ALEX
> Sabina!

>   SABINA
> (Astonished) Alex?

>   ALEX
> I need your help. I have to
> be on the other side of
> London - right now!

>   SABINA
> Why?

Well...what can he say? He has no time to
explain.

                    ALEX
           (Embarrassed) I have to
           save the world...?

And that makes complete sense to SABINA.

                    SABINA
           Right...

                                   CUT TO:

151 **INT.   JACK STARBRIGHT'S CAR (HYDE PARK)   DAY.** 151

JACK is talking on her cell phone.

                    JACK
           Can you put me through to
           Mrs. Jones? (Pause - then
           angry) I don't know what
           her first name is! I'm not
           sending her a birthday
           card! This is urgent!

JACK looks out of the front window of the car...

...just as a horse with SABINA PLEASURE
and ALEX RIDER leaps over the car hood and
gallops off through the park.

                                   CUT TO:

152 **EXT.   HYDE PARK, LONDON   DAY.**   152

SABINA has the reins. ALEX has SABINA, his
arms around her as they gallop forward
together.

ANOTHER ANGLE. The entire REGIMENT OF
HORSE GUARDS is out for the day, splendid
in their armor, hats, and uniforms. SABINA
and ALEX are heading right for them.

                    ALEX
           (Shouted) Keep going!

SABINA plows through them. Several SOL-
DIERS lose control. Their HORSES rear.

Two SOLDIERS come crashing to the ground.

The COMMANDER of the HORSE GUARDS sees what has happened. He is furious.

> COMMANDER
> After them!

The entire REGIMENT OF HORSE GUARDS chases after ALEX and SABINA.

ANOTHER ANGLE. ALEX looks around and sees that he's being pursued by the (Victorian) British army.

> ALEX
> (Shouted) Don't look round!

> SABINA
> (Shouted) Why not?

> ALEX
> (Shouted) Trust me...

They keep galloping. The HORSE GUARDS thunder after them.

ALEX and SABINA cross a road. The exit from the park is just ahead. The HORSE GUARDS are about to follow - but then a car suddenly appears, cutting them off. They come to an abrupt halt. More rearing HORSES. More falling SOLDIERS.

It is JACK. She smiles sweetly out of the open window.

> JACK
> Sorry!

ALEX and SABINA have gotten away.

                                    CUT TO:

153 **EXT.   LONDON - HYDE PARK CORNER   DAY.**   153

WIDE ANGLE. ALEX and SABINA gallop past the traffic that has come to a standstill at

this famous intersection. But they don't
need to stick to the roads...

They career across the grass and pass
through the ARCH itself. Then turn right
and head toward PICCADILLY.

The FLASH of a SPEED CAMERA, catching them
as they gallop past.

                                    CUT TO:

154 **EXT.   PICCADILLY CIRCUS   DAY.**   154

The bright lights of the ADVERTISING DIS-
PLAYS flicker above them as ALEX and SABINA
gallop through the heart of London.

                                    CUT TO:

155 **INT.   SAYLE TOWER - RECEPTION AREA   DAY.** 155

A harassed, panicking SAYLE comes bursting
through the glass doors and hurries across
the reception area. White marble and glass
all around. A SECURITY MAN, packed with
muscles, is on duty.

                    SAYLE
          If anyone comes in, kill
          them.

SAYLE charges into the elevator.

                                    CUT TO:

156 **INT.   SAYLE TOWER - SAYLE'S OFFICE   DAY.** 156

SAYLE approaches a complicated machine
attached to a mainframe computer. He turns it
on and feverishly begins to punch in codes.

                                    CUT TO:

157 **EXT.   SAYLE TOWER - ROOF   DAY.**   157

A landscape of curving glass. A section

splits open and slowly a radio transmitter
rises up. This is exactly the same transmitter
that ALEX saw when he was in Cornwall.

CUT TO:

158 **EXT.   CITY STREETS/SAYLE TOWER   DAY.**   158

The great dome of St. Paul's Cathedral rises up
above them. SABINA and ALEX gallop down a road
in the City of London. The horse makes a bizarre
contrast to the modern financial buildings.

ANOTHER ANGLE. They reach the SAYLE TOWER -
ALEX jumps off.

> ALEX
> Thanks, Sabina.

> SABINA
> Wait...!

But she's too late. ALEX has already gone.

CUT TO:

159 **INT.   SAYLE TOWER - RECEPTION AREA   DAY.**   159

The SECURITY MAN who greeted DARRIUS SAYLE
sees ALEX charge in through the glass doors.
He comes lumbering over.

ALEX sees he has a fight on his hands. But
there's no avoiding it. The SECURITY MAN grins
in a way that is barely human. He takes off his
security hat and spins it away (memories of
Oddjob) and takes a karate stance opposite ALEX.

ALEX sighs. How much more of this is there?

GIANT vs. KID in the wide expanse of the
reception area.

ALEX bows low. The correct way to begin a
fight.

The SECURITY MAN bows low and at that

moment ALEX kicks him once, hard, where it hurts. The SECURITY MAN crumples up. ALEX looks at him almost ruefully.

                    ALEX
          (Muttered) Schoolboy trick.

ALEX runs for the elevator.

                                        CUT TO:

160 **EXT.   SAYLE TOWER   DAY.**   160

SABINA has tied her horse to a traffic meter. She runs toward the glass doors of Sayle Tower.

                                        CUT TO:

161 **INT.   SAYLE TOWER - RECEPTION AREA   DAY.** 161

The SECURITY MAN is in a lot of pain. He staggers toward SABINA and tries to stop her.

                    SECURITY MAN
          Stop...

SABINA kicks him in exactly the same place that ALEX did and this time the SECURITY MAN is out of it. His face turns purple as he crumples a second time. SABINA heads for the elevator.

                                        CUT TO:

162 **INT.   SAYLE TOWER - SAYLE'S OFFICE   DAY.** 162

SAYLE feverishly waits for the machine to boot itself ready for transmission.

                                        CUT TO:

163 **EXT.   SAYLE TOWER - ROOF   DAY.**   163

The radio transmitter clicks into its final position. The radar dishes swivel, locking into the right frequency.

CUT TO:

164 **INT.   SAYLE TOWER - CORRIDOR   DAY.**   164

ALEX comes out of the elevator on the top
floor. He doesn't know where to go. He moves
quickly, quietly along a deserted corridor.
He comes to a service door. He opens it.
Ugly, metal stairs lead upward.

CUT TO:

165 **EXT.   LONDON STREETS   DAY.**   165

MI6 and POLICE VEHICLES speed through the
streets of London, heading from the Science
Museum to SAYLE TOWER.

CUT TO:

166 **INT./EXT.   MRS. JONES'S CAR/LONDON STREETS   DAY.**   166

MRS. JONES and ALAN BLUNT are sitting
together in the back of one of the cars.
Traffic all around. Sirens screaming.
They're tight-lipped...grim. BLUNT knows
that he should have thought of a back-up
system. Maybe they're going to be too
late.

CUT TO:

167 **INT./EXT.   JACK'S CAR/LONDON STREETS   DAY.**   167

JACK is also speeding in her slightly
grubby car toward SAYLE TOWER. But the
road ahead is blocked by a burst water
main. A WALL OF WATER stretches out in
front of her. A POLICEMAN is redirecting
the traffic.

JACK makes her decision. She speeds past
the POLICEMAN and straight toward the WALL
OF WATER.

Another angle as JACK bursts out the other
side. Her car is now gleaming clean.

CUT TO:

168 **INT.   SAYLE TOWER - SAYLE'S OFFICE   DAY.** 168

The machine is finally ready. A single command on the computer screen: ACTIVATE >.

SAYLE smiles to himself and stabs down. The
red button. The trigger.

But nothing happens. There's a soft whine
and the machine packs up. SAYLE scowls.
Then, instinctively, he looks up.

CUT TO:

169 **EXT.   SAYLE TOWER - ROOF   DAY.**   169

The service stairs have taken ALEX onto
the roof. He is holding a cable that he
has just pulled out of the radio transmitter, disabling it.

                    SAYLE
                (voice only)
         Put it back.

ANOTHER ANGLE. ALEX looks around to see
that SAYLE has also arrived on the roof.
SAYLE is holding a gun.

CUT TO:

170 **EXT.   SAYLE TOWER   DAY.**   170

A CLAMPING UNIT is looking at SABINA'S
HORSE, wondering where to fit the clamp.
Then a dozen cars scream past.

MI6 and POLICE screech to a halt from
all directions. MRS. JONES and BLUNT
get out of their car. JACK has also
arrived. She gets out of her car and
runs over to them.

                    JACK
         They're in there!

BLUNT
(To MRS. JONES) Take up
positions.

JACK
Don't you dare hurt them!

MI6 PEOPLE charge into Sayle Tower. Other
ARMED SOLDIERS are heading into offices
across the street.

CUT TO:

171 **EXT.   SAYLE TOWER   DAY.**   171

SAYLE has a gun on ALEX. The loose cable
(with an attachment where it slots into the
transmitter) is in ALEX'S hand.

ALEX
It's all over, Sayle. You've
got nowhere else to go.

SAYLE
Put it back!

ALEX
No.

SAYLE

Then I will...

A pause. SAYLE fires the gun. Still holding the cable, ALEX dives for cover behind
the radio transmitter. SAYLE fires again
and again.

The glass roof has a steep curve. ALEX
begins to roll. The bullets ricochet around
him. ALEX is rolling faster. Suddenly he
sees the danger. If he doesn't stop, he's
going to roll over the edge and down, fifty
stories, to his death.

He doesn't stop. But he's still holding the
cable. He goes over the edge. The cable

goes with him. ALEX is launched into space. Only the cable saves him.

Still holding the gun, SAYLE walks toward him.

CUT TO:

172 **EXT.   LONDON OFFICES   DAY.**   172

MI6 MARKSMEN have reached the offices surrounding SAYLE TOWER. They take up positions.

An MI6 MARKSMAN speaks into his radio.

> SPECIAL FORCES MARKSMAN
> I can see them! I can take them out...

CUT TO:

173 **EXT.   SAYLE TOWER   DAY.**   173

BLUNT has received the message. MRS. JONES and JACK STARBRIGHT are with him.

> SPECIAL FORCES MARKSMAN
> (voice only)
> The kid has the cable. He's got a transmitter on the roof.

> BLUNT
> Fire on my command.

> JACK
> No! You're going to hit Alex.

> BLUNT
> This isn't just about Alex.

> JACK
> (Dismayed) What?

> BLUNT
> (Into radio) Prepare to fire.

And this is the moment when MRS. JONES finally takes control.

                    MRS. JONES
        No. Wait...

                    BLUNT
        Mrs. Jones...I really don't
        think this is the time for
        an argument.

                    MRS. JONES
        There is no argument.

A pause. Is BLUNT going to lose it? NO -
he realizes that for once he might be
wrong. With something approaching a
courteous smile, he hands the transmitter to MRS. JONES.

                                    CUT TO:

174 **EXT.   LONDON OFFICES   DAY.**   174

The MI6 MARKSMEN take aim at the figures on
the roof.

                                    CUT TO:

175 **INT.   SAYLE TOWER - CORRIDOR   DAY.**   175

MI6 PEOPLE charge out of the elevator on
the top floor. One of them receives a radio
command from MRS. JONES.

                    MI6 MAN
        We're to stand by...

Everyone freezes.

                                    CUT TO:

176 **EXT.   SAYLE TOWER - ROOF   DAY.**   176

ALEX is dangling from the cable, fifty stories above London. SAYLE smiles...

...then cries out as he is grabbed from
behind. It's SABINA PLEASURE. She's
somehow made it to the roof and now she

and SAYLE struggle as ALEX dangles below.

                              CUT TO:

177 **EXT.   SAYLE TOWER   DAY.**   177

MRS. JONES speaks urgently into her radio mike.

                    MRS. JONES
          Who is it? Tell me what's
          happening...

                              CUT TO:

178 **EXT.   SAYLE TOWER - ROOF   DAY.**   178

SAYLE gets the better of SABINA. He swings her around and...

...throws her off the edge of the roof!!!

SABINA screams.

                              CUT TO:

179 **EXT.   SAYLE TOWER   DAY.**   179

A shocked reaction from MRS. JONES, ALAN BLUNT, and JACK, all craning their necks upward...

                              CUT TO:

180 **EXT.   SAYLE TOWER - ROOF   DAY.**   180

...and then relief. ALEX RIDER catches SABINA - her hand in his hand - as she falls.

So now ALEX is dangling with one hand attached to the cable. SABINA is hanging below him, her hand in his, terrified. There's a one-hundred-meter fall below them.

JACK STARBRIGHT, ALAN BLUNT, and MRS. JONES are at sidewalk level. MI6 MEN are everywhere.

And DARRIUS SAYLE is on the roof, just above ALEX and SABINA. A man with nothing to lose. He walks forward and hovers over them.

SAYLE raises the gun.

> SAYLE
> You know what got me? What really got me was them sending a kid. A man I could have dealt with. Oh well. This is where it ends. Good-bye...

He takes aim. SABINA stares helplessly. ALEX waits for the end.

And then, appearing out of nowhere, huge, silent. A HELICOPTER. It rises up as if from the street. Suddenly it fills the screen.

YASSEN GREGOROVICH isn't the pilot. He's sitting behind an open door. He's carrying a high-velocity rifle. SAYLE sees him. For a moment we think YASSEN is going to kill ALEX.

YASSEN fires three times.

QUICK CUTS. We don't know who's been hit. Is it ALEX? No. He's fine. SABINA? The same. SAYLE. A strange smile - and then he falls backward off the roof.

                                    CUT TO:

181 **EXT.   SAYLE TOWER   DAY.**   181

JACK STARBRIGHT turns away as the body falls.

                                    CUT TO:

182 **EXT.   SAYLE TOWER - ROOF   DAY.**   182

The helicopter hovers. ALEX is still dangling. The wind rushes all around him. And

SABINA can't hold on much longer. Worse
than that (can this get worse?), the cable
is beginning to come away from the wall.

ALEX sees a set of windows with a balcony.

> ALEX
> Sabina...I'm going to try to
> swing you onto the balcony.

> SABINA
> Don't! The cable will break!

> ALEX
> I can do it.

A pause. And a brief, romantic moment. The
beginning of young love?

> ALEX
> Do you trust me?

> SABINA
> No.

The end of young love. ALEX swings her.
Once. Twice. On the third time, he lets go.
SABINA flies through the air and lands on
the balcony. She's safe.

But the movement causes part of the cable
to break free. ALEX plunges down about ten
meters. Now he's below the balcony.
There's no chance he can make it.

ANOTHER ANGLE. More pins holding the cable
break free. It's obvious that the cable is
about to snap.

ALEX dangles. Utterly helpless.

The helicopter rises above him.

CLOSE ON ALEX as he tries to climb back up
the cable. But it's too thin.

PULLING BACK. A hand suddenly extends

itself downward. YASSEN GREGOROVICH has left the helicopter on a winch.

He's upside down, holding out his hand. There's a similarity between this and the moment when IAN RIDER died.

>   YASSEN
>   You need a hand?

ALEX is unsure what to do. This is the man he most hates and fears. The man who killed his uncle. But what choice does he have? The cable is giving way.

The moment of truth.

ALEX can't risk waiting any longer. He takes YASSEN'S hand.

>   CUT TO:

183 **EXT.   SAYLE TOWER   DAY.**   183

BLUNT (in radio contact), MRS. JONES, and JACK STARBRIGHT are down below. They see the helicopter tilt and accelerate away over the London skyline.

>   CUT TO:

184 **EXT.   DISTANT LONDON ROOFTOP   DAY.**   184

The helicopter is parked on the top of another, older building. The PILOT is waiting. YASSEN GREGOROVICH and ALEX face each other. London stretches out below.

>   ALEX
>   Why?

>   YASSEN
>   Sayle had become an embarrass-
>   ment to the people I work for.

>   ALEX
>   What about me?

                    YASSEN
          I had no instructions con-
          cerning you.

A pause.

                    ALEX
          This doesn't change any-
          thing. You killed my uncle.
          You're still my enemy.

                    YASSEN
          I have a lot of enemies.

                    ALEX
          This isn't over.

                    YASSEN
          I think it is, Alex. Go
          back to school. You don't
          belong to my world. You
          should forget about me.

                    ALEX
          (Threatening) I'll never
          forget you.

YASSEN glances at ALEX.

                    YASSEN
          That's your choice.

YASSEN turns and walks toward the helicopter.

ANOTHER ANGLE. ALEX stands, alone and very
solitary, on the rooftop as the helicopter leaves. It circles over him once,
then, as ALEX watches, it flies off into
the setting sun.

                              FADE TO:

185 **EXT.   BROOKLAND SCHOOL   DAY.**   185

JACK STARBRIGHT walks with ALEX to school.
The start of another ordinary day. Lots of
other KIDS and TEACHERS arriving.

                    ALEX
          You don't have to walk with
          me to school.

                    JACK
          I just want to make sure
          you get there, Alex. You
          know. After what happened.

The PE TEACHER notices ALEX.

And JACK notices the PE TEACHER. Immediate
attraction. On both sides. The PE TEACHER
smiles at JACK and moves on.

                    JACK
          (To ALEX) Who's he? How
          come you never mentioned
          him to me before?

ALEX smiles. Some things never change. Then
he joins the stream of KIDS going into
school.

ANOTHER ANGLE. In the distance, GARY is on
his bike, leaning against a tree and trying to chat up SABINA.

SABINA sees ALEX arrive and, ignoring GARY,
runs over to him.

                    SABINA
          Alex!

In the background, virtually unnoticed,
GARY loses his balance and, with his bicycle, topples sideways to the ground. JACK
and TEACHER are exchanging phone numbers.

SABINA throws her arms around ALEX and
kisses him. Not a cool thing to do in a
school yard.

                    ALEX
          (Embarrassed) Sabina! Don't
          do that!

ALEX and SABINA walk toward the first class.

> SABINA
> They made me sign the
> Official Secrets Act. I'm
> not allowed to tell anyone
> what happened.

> ALEX
> Me too.

> SABINA
> Are you really a spy?

> ALEX
> No.

> SABINA
> That's not what they told me.

> ALEX
> I'm not a spy. It's not going
> to happen again.

> SABINA
> (Doubtful) No.

> ALEX
> No. I'm just me.

SABINA takes his arm. They walk into the distance.

ANOTHER ANGLE. The CAMERA whips up the roof of a nearby building. ALEX is being watched by a FIGURE in SPECIAL FORCES or police combat gear. The FIGURE is using some sort of hi-tech camera/surveillance device.

We see ALEX through the device. Numbers and measurements along the sides of the screen.

His next enemy? Or MI6 sizing him up for his next mission? Either way, it isn't over yet...

                                    CUT TO BLACK

THE GAME IS ON.

ALEX RIDER
STORMBREAKER

PLAY THE GAME ON

NINTENDO DS ™ **GAME BOY ADVANCE**

Making Sure seriously ill kids and teens never have to feel alone

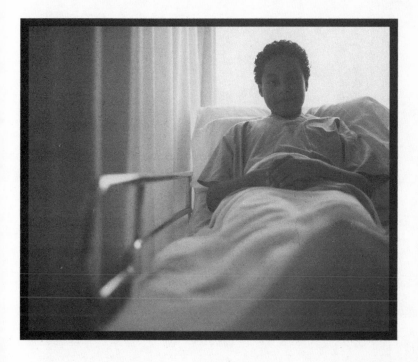

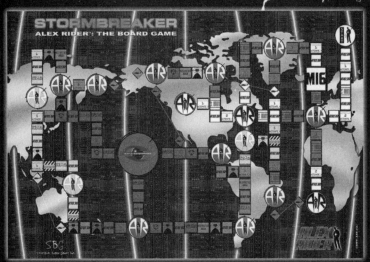